WED IN DISGRACE

CONVENIENT ARRANGEMENTS (BOOK 3)

ROSE PEARSON

LANDON HILL MEDIA

WED IN DISGRACE

Convenient Arrangements

(Book 3)

By

Rose Pearson

WED IN DISGRACE

PROLOGUE

"*I suppose now that I have no other choice but to take you into my home. However, it shall not be of long duration, for I intend to find a suitable match for you for soon.*"

Miss Delilah Johnston sat down heavily on her bed, the letter falling from her hands to the floor. Tears flooded her vision as she tried her best to keep her composure.

It had been some years since she had last heard from her uncle. Her uncle who had inherited her father's title when he had died, leaving Delilah without father or mother. Even though she had been entitled to her time of mourning, her uncle had refused to allow her that and had shipped her to a school where she had been meant to receive all the education that would then make her a very suitable and elegant young lady. Whilst that had happened, Delilah had found no happiness. There had been rules to follow; stark, strict rules that allowed for not even the smallest infringement. Punishments had been severe for even the slightest misdemeanor and Delilah had often had to go without luncheon and dinner in the hope that this would teach her what was expected. The established ladies, as they were known, ruled with an iron rod and Delilah had become weary under their cruel ways.

"Miss Delilah?"

She turned her head swiftly to see the only friend she had ever made at the decrepit place. "Betty," she said, as the maid came a little further into the room. "Are you quite all right?"

Betty glanced around as though making quite certain that there was no one else around—no one who might inform those in charge that she had been speaking to Delilah.

"Your letter," she said, gesturing to the one on the floor. "It does not make you happy?"

Delilah shook her head. "No," she said dully. "It does not."

"Then, you are to stay here?"

Slowly, Delilah shook her head, her heart aching in her chest. "I am to return to my uncle. He does not intend to keep me in his household for long, however. It seems I am to be wed."

Betty caught her breath, and Delilah looked up at her miserably.

"Indeed," she said heavily. "It will not be a match of my choosing, of course. It will be someone that I do not know and certainly do not care for. In fact, I am certain that my uncle will choose the very worst sort of gentleman and push me towards him, given how little he seems to care for me." Her heart continued to ache as she turned her head to look down at her letter, her eyes filling with fresh tears. "I do not know what I shall do."

Biting her lip, Betty came a little closer to Delilah, her expression one of concern. Looking steadily down at Delilah, she put one hand on her shoulder. Their friendship had formed over the years Delilah had been there, and whilst there was a great difference in their status, Delilah had found Betty to be a very loyal friend indeed.

A sudden idea came into Delilah's mind and she caught her breath, looking up at Betty.

"You should come with me, Betty," she breathed, reaching up to catch Betty's hand. "You could be my lady's maid."

Betty's eyes flared, staring down at Delilah with astonishment.

"My uncle would not be able to refuse you," Delilah continued, her heart thundering with sudden hope. "If I am a proper young lady, I require a lady's maid, do I not?"

Betty, it seemed, did not know what to say, for she continued to hold Delilah's gaze for a long time, nothing being said.

"I know you do not like it here," Delilah continued, pressing Betty's hand with great fervor. "You could come with me, could be my lady's maid and continue with me into my married life." She gestured to the large, sparse room which held nothing more than a few beds and bedside tables and drawers. "I am sure that my uncle's house—and my husband's house, whoever he might turn out to be—will have a better establishment than this."

Pressing her lips together, Betty considered for a few more minutes as Delilah waited desperately to hear her friend's answer. It was a very foolish idea in some respects, for to steal Betty away from what was her current employment without the assurance that she would then be given a suitable position with suitable pay was quite ridiculous, but Delilah could barely think of leaving her friend behind here.

"I need my pay, Miss Delilah," Betty said with a shake of her head. "I cannot survive without it."

Delilah nodded, desperation flooding her. "But a lady's maid would be given payment, would she not?" she said, grasping Betty's hand. "And you would have a warm bed and food. And...and...if I find that you are not given the pay expected, I will make certain that you are reimbursed in some way." Realizing how desperate she sounded, Delilah closed her eyes, shook her head, and let go of Betty's hand. There was no assurance for Betty in this situation. It was selfishness that wanted her to accompany her as a lady's maid: selfishness that wanted to keep Betty by her side.

"I am sorry, Betty," she mumbled, keeping her eyes closed as shame began to fill her. "I should not even have *thought* of such a thing. It is foolish of me to do so, for I cannot promise you a single thing."

"I—I think I will come with you."

Delilah's eyes flew open, and she stared at Betty in shock.

"I cannot even promise you that you will be paid, Betty!" she exclaimed as though she was now trying to dissuade her. "What if—"

"I do not like working here, Miss Delilah," Betty interrupted, putting one hand out, her palm forward to quieten her protests. "When you first asked me, I was a little taken aback, but now..." She nodded her head as though reassuring herself. "Yes, I will come with you, Miss Delilah."

Delilah did not know what to say, warring between relief and fear. She had spoken hastily and now worried that Betty might be thrown from her uncle's house without employment or reference.

You shall have to be strong, Delilah, she told herself as Betty began to smile. *You will have to insist on keeping Betty if she is to come with you. She is now trusting you for her future employment.*

"Think about it a little longer, Betty," she said slowly rising to her feet and facing the maid. "I spoke quickly and I—"

"When do you have to leave?" Betty asked as Delilah bent down to pick up her letter. "Is it soon?"

Delilah nodded. "Within the sennight," she said quietly. "My uncle is sending a carriage on Friday evening."

Betty considered for a moment, then smiled. "Then I shall be waiting," she said, a bright look in her eyes. "I am sure that the established ladies of this school will not be waiting by the carriage door to wave you away!"

Despite the sorrow that was in this statement, Delilah could not help but smile, albeit ruefully. "No, I do not think they will."

"Then I will be ready just to steal away," Betty said, speaking in a very matter-of-fact manner. "I do not think they will allow me just to leave, so I will have to slip past them in the darkness."

The sadness and pain that had filled Delilah's heart ever since she had read the letter from her uncle began to lift as Betty's sudden excitement began to fill the room.

"You will have to be careful," Delilah said as Betty beamed at her before glancing all around the room again in case someone was about to come in and see them. "The established ladies will not allow you to leave if they see you."

Betty laughed and shook her head. "They do not see me even when I am very close to them," she said, backing away towards the door. "I am *certain* they will not see me on Friday evening, either."

DELILAH HAD BEEN QUITE correct in her assumptions that none of the established ladies would come to bid her farewell. The carriage was ready and waiting for her, but she had to carry her own cases to the carriage. No one came to assist her; no one came to ensure that she made her way to the transport safely. Only the driver climbed down—begrudgingly—from his perch to lift her cases onto the top.

"They didn't even offer me anything," he grumbled as Delilah placed the last of her things down, shivering in the cold wind. "Not even a glass of water."

"I—I am sorry about that," Delilah stammered, a little uncertain as to what else she could offer. "I would be glad to stop somewhere for a little refreshment if that would be of use."

The driver said nothing, looking at her steadily in the gloom as her glance darted to the ground and then back to his face, uncertain as to whether or not he thought her foolish.

"That is kind of you, miss," he said after a few moments. "I certainly would be grateful for it."

She offered him a slightly tentative smile, the moonlight highlighting his craggy features. He set her case down again and, with a small inclination of his head, opened the carriage door for her.

"Thank you," Delilah murmured, stepping inside quickly so that he might shut the door again. Letting out a long breath, she settled back against the squabs and tried not to allow her anxious nerves to take a complete hold of her.

"Good evening, Miss Delilah."

A shriek came to her lips, but Delilah stifled it with a great effort. She had not even heard the carriage door on her right open, and certainly had not seen Betty climbing inside.

"I am sorry, Miss," Betty whispered, her whole being almost entirely shrouded in black. "I did not mean to startle you."

"Betty," Delilah breathed as the driver finished hefting the cases onto the top of the carriage and climbed back up onto his seat, the carriage shifting right and left, squeaking as it did so. "I am so grateful for your willingness to come with me."

The carriage began to roll forward, and Delilah let

out a long, slow breath, her eyes closing tightly. "They are not chasing after you it seems."

"No," Betty chuckled, pushing down the hood of a thick, black cloak that Delilah had never seen before. "I told you that the established ladies never really pay me much attention. They will begin to notice when the work is not done, however, but that will not be for a day or so."

Delilah nodded to herself, attempting to allow this to reassure her. "And they have not shown any interest in discovering the whereabouts of my uncle's residence."

Leaning across the carriage, Betty clasped Delilah's hand. "You need not worry, Miss Delilah," she said firmly. "I do not intend to go back there or to leave your side, no matter what your uncle might think."

"You have more bravery than I," Delilah answered honestly, "but I cannot express to you just how grateful I am for your company, Betty. It means so much to me."

Clouds began to cover the moon, and the flickers of light that had come into the carriage began to fade away. Delilah closed her eyes and rested her head back, feeling both anxiety and relief. Relief that she was gone from the school but fear as to what might now be waiting for her at her uncle's house. Just what sort of gentleman would he force her to wed? And would she have strength enough to face whatever was waiting for her once she returned to the only home she had ever known?

CHAPTER ONE

"Miss Delilah. Miss Delilah!"

Delilah groaned groggily as a firm hand shook her awake. Wincing, she tried to open her eyes but found them heavy, her whole body aching.

"We are in London, Miss Delilah!"

"London?"

She was awake in a moment, staring all around her as she looked at the great buildings, the many carriages that went by her on the other side.

"I am sure it is London," Betty said with a twist of excitement in her voice. "I was here before, before I was employed by the school. I am certain that we are in London!"

Delilah swallowed hard, straightening a little more as she realized where she was going. Her father had once had a townhouse in London, which her uncle had obviously inherited. This must be where they were to go, meaning that it was, most likely, the start of the Season. Delilah had never been to London for the Season before but had certainly heard of it from her father and from some of the other ladies that had been in the school.

"The gentleman my uncle intends me to marry must be in London," she whispered, sitting back as her heart began to pound frantically, sweat beading on her brow. "Oh, Betty, I am so very afraid." The last time she had seen her uncle, he had been a great, looming figure, practically throwing her into the carriage that would take her to the school. She had wept and cried every moment of that journey, broken over the loss of her parents and the sudden appearance of this cruel uncle in their place.

"Your uncle is not a good man?" Betty asked gently.

"No," Delilah answered, her voice shaking. "I do not think he is. I am afraid of what he will do and, given that I am his charge, there is very little I can do."

Betty reached across and pressed her hand. "I am sure you will find enough courage, Miss Delilah."

"I must hope so," she answered, wishing she had any form of strength in place of the weakness that pulled at her. The carriage continued on its journey towards her uncle's townhouse, and Delilah concentrated on breathing slowly, closing her eyes and forcing her fear down.

"Look, Miss Delilah!"

Delilah opened her eyes to see the carriage beginning to move towards a grand townhouse. Delilah had never been to London before and so she did not know what her late father's townhouse looked like—but it was not the townhouse that Betty had pointed out. Instead, Delilah's attention was drawn towards a gentleman standing on the stone steps—but just in front of him, her head held high as though she were someone with a good deal of status and grandeur, stood an older lady with gray hair and a sharpness to her eyes that sent fear into Delilah's heart.

"I do not know who she is," Delilah whispered, her hands pressed to her heart. "I do not think that I have ever seen her before."

"Is she your uncle's wife?" Betty asked, but Delilah shook her head no. There was no time to ask anything more, for the carriage came to a stop and the door opened for her.

Taking in a deep breath and praying that she would not give the appearance of weakness, Delilah climbed out of the carriage carefully and came to stand at the bottom of the stone steps. She did not look at her uncle but kept her eyes averted, as she knew he would expect.

"What is that?"

Her uncle's voice was harsh, twisting cruelly as he spoke. Delilah dared a glance at him and saw that he was looking at Betty.

"She is my lady's maid, Uncle," she said, relieved that her voice did not shake. "That is all."

Her uncle snorted. "Get rid of her. You have no need for her."

"Do not be so foolish, Denholm."

Delilah's eyes flared in surprise as the older lady swung about to face Lord Denholm, her hands planted firmly on her hips.

"The girl needs a lady's maid. You know that as well as me."

"I have already employed one," Lord Denholm sniffed, but the older lady simply laughed.

"Then you shall find her other employment, given that your niece has one of her own already," the lady said, swinging herself back around and coming down the steps towards Delilah.

"Delilah," she said, reaching out to grasp Delilah's hand and speaking to her with a warmth that she had not expected. "I am sure you do not remember me but I am your godmother."

The shock that rolled over Delilah almost knocked her to the ground. Her godmother?

"When I heard of your mother's death, I came to meet with you and your father," the lady continued, gently. "Your father was so lost in grief that he did not want to allow me to continue visiting you. And then, when he passed away, I felt it my duty to go to you." Her eyes narrowed, and she shot a glance back towards Lord Denholm. "But I was a little too late."

"You have no claim over her!" Lord Denholm shouted, his voice sharp. "As I have informed you time and time again!"

"But," the lady continued, clearly ignoring Lord Denholm, "I have not given up. And when I heard that your uncle was back in London, I knew that he would be bringing you back here. Therefore, I have determined to remain close to you throughout the Season so that the burden on your uncle is not so great." Her eyes twinkled, her lips quirking, making it quite apparent that this was not the main reason for her presence here in London. "Your uncle will find, Miss Delilah, that I am not easily dissuaded from my intentions."

Blinking rapidly, Delilah tried to take all of this in. "I

do not understand," she said, closing her eyes tightly. "You have come to help me?"

"To be your godmother," the lady said emphatically. "Now, do come in. I will help you unpack and rest before it is time to meet with your uncle."

Delilah found her arm linked with the older lady's as she was led up the stone steps, Betty at her heels. Her uncle, for a moment, did not look as though he would move out of her way, but, at a sharp glance from the lady, he stepped aside. Delilah looked up into his face, seeing the dark brows settled over a pair of cold blue eyes, lines grooved deeply into his forehead, his lips thin and curled on one side as a sneer formed. He was just as intimidating as she remembered him.

"I—I do not know your name," she whispered as though she would be in difficulty merely for speaking aloud. "Might I inquire as to what it is?"

The lady glanced towards her, smiling. "Lady Newfield," she said, leading Delilah towards the stair-case. "And as I have said, I am your godmother and *very* pleased to have found you again. Particularly at a time such as this!"

"Lady Newfield," Delilah murmured, feeling incredibly grateful for the lady's presence. "You cannot know what this means, to have you here at this time."

Lady Newfield said nothing but led her into a room a little along the hallway at the top of the stairs, clearly having been in this house before.

"And I must thank you also for insisting that Betty remain with me," Delilah continued as she glanced behind her at the maid, who was looking all around her with wide eyes. "I will confess the truth to you, Lady Newfield. I—"

"Betty is your lady's maid, and that is all that matters," Lady Newfield said with a firmness in her voice. "And if you have both managed to make an escape from that dreadful school your uncle sent you to, Delilah, then I am very glad indeed for you both."

Seeing that Lady Newfield already knew what Delilah had been trying to explain, Delilah managed a small smile as she walked into what was now her room, looking all around it.

"It is not quite as large as I would have expected for you," Lady Newfield said, looking about the room with an air of dissatisfaction. "But it will do."

"It is much larger than I have had before," Delilah murmured, sitting down in a chair by the fireplace and shivering slightly. "Although it is a trifle cold."

"But we are used to the cold," Betty said briskly as she began to unpack some of Delilah's things. "I am sure that—"

Lady Newfield tsked. "Your uncle should have laid a fire in this room if it has sat unused for a long duration," she said, clearly irritated. "Have no fear, Delilah; we shall be warm again very soon." She rang the bell with firm hand and Delilah felt herself shrink, afraid that her uncle would come into the room in a furious temper and demand to know why she had rung the bell.

"You need not be so afraid," Lady Newfield said practically, sitting down opposite her and looking at her with such a firm gaze that Delilah felt as though she was being chided. "Your uncle may be intimidating and cruel, but you are not alone in this."

"But I am to be wed to a gentleman of his choosing," Delilah replied, with a sudden lump in her throat as she fought back tears. "I do not want to be but he—"

"And that is something we cannot ignore nor change," Lady Newfield said, reaching across the space between them and putting her hand on Delilah's knee. "But I will be with you throughout and will encourage you in all things."

Despite her best efforts, a tear fell to Delilah's cheek. "But what if my husband is cruel?" she whispered, envisioning another gentleman very similar to her uncle. "Whatever shall I do?"

Lady Newfield smiled gently. "I will be there with you," she said, not providing Delilah with any particular answer but reassuring her, nonetheless. "And I shall do what I can to influence your uncle, but I do not think that he will be willing to change his mind if a specific gentleman is his particular choice."

This was gently said, but it held the truth that Delilah well understood. Her fears were still very great indeed, but she allowed herself to gain a little courage from Lady Newfield's presence, almost instinctively knowing that she could trust this lady with all that was to happen.

"So," Lady Newfield continued in a practical voice. "You are to attend your first ball of the Season tomorrow and I have ensured that I will be present and waiting for your arrival."

Delilah nodded, her lips pressed together as she nodded, trying to do all she could to remain strong.

"I am not certain as to whether or not you will be introduced to this gentleman tomorrow evening," Lady Newfield continued with a hardness about her mouth as she looked away, "but if you are, I shall be there, standing alongside you, making certain that this gentleman knows that I have no intention of disappearing from your life even when you are a married woman."

"That is very kind of you, Lady Newfield," Delilah said, one hand pressed lightly against her stomach as she rose to stand tall, knowing now that her uncle was expecting her. "I am very glad you are here."

"I am only sorry I was not able to be present with you earlier," Lady Newfield replied, getting to her feet. "Now, we are to go and sit with your uncle for a time, I believe." One eyebrow lifted, and her lips quirked. "Let us hope that there will be tea, for I am in desperate need of sustenance already!"

Delilah managed to smile as Lady Newfield led her to the door. She threw a look back at Betty, who nodded and smiled, continuing to unpack Delilah's things as though she had always done so. Her heart still pounding furiously in her chest, Delilah walked after Lady Newfield, looking all about the townhouse and trying to imagine her father living there. Pain sliced through her as she recalled the many happy times they had enjoyed together back at her father's estate. To lose him so suddenly—for he had unexpectedly had great pains in his chest, which had led to him taking his last few breaths of life—had been torturous to witness and all the more painful thereafter when she had realized he would not be returning to her. When her uncle had come to take over the estate, his title now the same as her father's had once been, Delilah had not known what to expect. She had prayed that her uncle would be kind, that he would understand the pain and grief that had racked her, but her prayers had not been answered. He had marched into the estate and had changed her life forever.

"You must not be afraid of your uncle, Delilah," Lady Newfield murmured as they began to descend the stairs. "And even if you are afraid, then I must ask for you to do all you can to hide your fear."

Delilah opened her mouth to ask why, only to close it again.

"You can understand why that is," Lady Newfield said with a knowing look. "Your uncle will use your fear against you. It will give him an increased sense of control over you if you show him that you are fearful of him."

"I understand," Delilah answered honestly. "I shall do all I can to remain strong in the face of his callousness."

"I know that he has been more than unkind to you," Lady Newfield said. "But that was at a time when you were grieving, when you were in the depths of sorrow. I cannot imagine what you must have endured, being sent away and knowing that you did not have either your mother or your father any longer."

A sob lodged in Delilah's throat, and she did not answer, shaking her head instead.

"Lord Denholm clearly did not want the burden of you any longer," Lady Newfield said with steel in her eyes. "But I certainly do, Delilah, and I promise you that no matter what you are faced with, you shall not have to do so alone any longer."

It was this courage that brought Delilah a little hope as she walked into the drawing-room to find her uncle standing at the mantlepiece, his brows lowered over his eyes, his hands held firmly behind his back. His eyes were like flint, watching her as she came into the room and never once looking away. With fear still blossoming in her heart, she bobbed a quick curtsy and then sat down. Lady Newfield did not curtsy but rather marched to a chair next to Delilah and took a seat.

"Delilah." Lord Denholm's voice was low and rough. "You know why you have been returned to London."

Delilah wanted to remain silent, not quite sure she could trust her voice. Breathing out slowly, she nodded, only to catch Lady Newfield's eye. With a deep breath, she lifted her chin a little more and looked at her uncle.

"Yes, Uncle," she said, aware that her voice trembled but doing all she could to speak with as much firmness as she could muster. "I am to be married."

Her uncle flinched as though he had not expected her to speak so. "Yes, that is so," he grated. "I will not tell you the name of the gentleman as yet, for I do not think that such a thing is necessary at this time."

Lady Newfield let out a huff of breath. "Do not be so foolish, Denholm," she said abruptly, gesturing furiously. "If she is to meet the gentleman tomorrow at the ball, then why should you not give her his name at present?"

Lord Denholm drew himself up. "I do not think that

this is any of your business, Lady Newfield," he said with great dignity. "After all, you—"

"I am to be accompanying Delilah through the Season, as you well know," Lady Newfield interrupted, her voice ringing out across the room. "Given that she has no mother to guide her, as well as the fact that you have no real interest in doing anything other than marrying her off to whomever you have chosen, you can, at the very least, inform the girl as to who her husband will be!"

Lord Denholm gritted his teeth, anger burning in his eyes, and Delilah felt herself shrink away, daring to look at Lady Newfield and expecting her to be doing the same as she.

However, Lady Newfield's back was straight, head up and her gaze fixed to Lord Denholm. Her eyes were blazing, her chin lifted and her hands tight on the arms of the chair. It was clear that she had no fear when it came to Lord Denholm and that, Delilah realized, was the sort of courage she wished she could have.

"I do not think it necessary," Lord Denholm snapped, his eyes hard. "But given that your *godmother* insists..." The word was spoken with venom and Delilah felt herself shudder, hating the feeling that came with it. "I shall do what she has asked."

"Good," Lady Newfield retorted, sitting back in her chair a little more. "It is the very least that your niece deserves."

Even when she had gained what she had wanted, Lady Newfield did not remain silent. She had every intention of showing Lord Denholm that she was not someone who would hide from him and remain silent and obedient as he hoped. Delilah herself kept quiet, finding it difficult enough to look directly into her uncle's face but forcing herself to do so regardless.

"An arrangement has been made with a gentleman of the *ton*," Lord Denholm said with a tight smile that looked almost like a snarl. "He does not require a great dowry—which is just as well given that you have very little."

Delilah closed her eyes for a moment, a shudder running through her. She knew that she had once had an excellent dowry, and certainly did not think that her father would have removed it from her before he had passed away. Which meant, as far as she was concerned, that her uncle had taken some of it for himself, reducing her value significantly.

"The gentleman is an earl, with excellent connections, a good amount of wealth, and an eagerness to ensure that his family line continues," Lord Denholm finished as though this should satisfy Delilah's curiosity. "You will give him what he desires."

"And in return, you are to gain something from him, I suppose," Lady Newfield said sharply. "Might I ask what it is?"

Lord Denholm's eyes glittered. "There is nothing that I am to gain," he snapped, although Delilah was certain he did not tell the truth. "The gentleman is to meet you for the first time tomorrow evening, and all shall go from there."

"Might I ask what that entails?" Delilah found herself asking, her breathing a little tight as she tried to speak to her uncle without fear. "Do you expect us to become engaged immediately?"

Her uncle opened his mouth but glanced at Lady Newfield before closing it again. When he finally spoke, it was with consideration.

"I should prefer it to be at once," he said, his lip curling. "But Lady Newfield insists that there is a short time of courtship beforehand, and thus, I have agreed."

Delilah frowned, wondering what it was that had Lady Newfield speaking so openly and being able to demand so much from Lord Denholm. Yes, she had a very strong presence indeed, but that could not be all that was pushing Lord Denholm to do as she requested.

"The name of this gentleman, Lord Denholm?" Again, Lady Newfield's voice was filled with authority, and Lord Denholm frowned harder than before, his brows knotting into a dark line.

"Very well, Lady Newfield!" he grated. "It is the Earl of Coventry."

This name meant nothing to Delilah, but to Lady Newfield, it evidently meant a great deal. She clutched at her heart, her eyes flaring wide and a gasp escaping her. Delilah's heart began to hammer furiously as she saw the paleness of Lady Newfield's cheeks and began to fear that this gentleman, this unknown fellow she was to marry, might in fact be even worse than her uncle was at present.

"I think that is all I have to say at present," Lord Denholm said, clearly using the silence from Lady Newfield and the shock of his words to escape. "Tea will be served to you now, and dinner will be sent to you in your room, Delilah. I am sure you will need to rest."

Delilah said nothing, nausea swirling through her as she watched her uncle leave. Lady Newfield said nothing for some minutes, although her lips were now pursed and her hand pressed to her cheek as though she were attempting to warm herself a little.

"Lady Newfield?" Delilah tried, a little timidly. "What is wrong?" Sweat broke out on her brow. "Is my husband a cruel man?"

Lady Newfield closed her eyes tightly before turning towards Delilah. "Did your uncle say there was to be tea?" she said, her voice flat. "I think we need to have something before I explain all to you."

This did not satisfy Delilah, who did not want to wait any longer but rather wanted to hear all that Lady Newfield had to say. However, the maid came in at precisely that moment, and a tray was set down for them both. Delilah did not feel able to refuse. Serving the tea as quickly as she could and refusing Lady Newfield's encouragement to eat one of the honey cakes, she sat back down again and fixed her eyes steadily upon her godmother.

"How is it that you are able to have such an influence on my uncle, Lady Newfield?" Delilah asked, thinking that mayhap the lady would be willing to answer this question before speaking to her of her soon-to-be husband. "He appears unable to refuse you on so many things."

Lady Newfield's eyes flickered, her brows lowering. "Your uncle is not a good man, Delilah, as you well know," she said calmly, putting her teacup down. "I may have discovered something about his behavior that I know for certain he would not want to be shared with anyone else."

Rather surprised, Delilah nodded but did not say anything more.

"He does not like me at all," Lady Newfield continued with a wave of her hand, "but I confess that I knew I had to have something by which I could influence his behavior." Her eyes narrowed. "I know that you are desperate to ask me about the earl, Delilah, but I fear it may be too much for you. You have endured a great deal already today."

Trying to summon the strength that Lady Newfield had asked her to seek, Delilah shook her head. "Please, Lady Newfield," she said urgently. "I *must* know. I do not think I can wait here in confusion and worry, not knowing what the problem is with my betrothed."

Lady Newfield said nothing but took a sip of her tea, studying Delilah carefully.

"I do not want to upset you," she said slowly. "I can now understand why your uncle is so eager to have you wed so soon—and what benefits will be given him because of it."

"Oh?"

Lady Newfield shook her head. "Lord Coventry, whilst he might be an earl, has been somewhat...set aside by society." She shook her head. "That is not to say that he will not be invited to further gatherings and occasions, of course, because society is fickle and there is some confusion over what it is that he has done."

This sounded ominous and Delilah swallowed hard, setting her teacup down. "What is it that he has done, Lady Newfield?"

"I was not fully aware of it, and to be frank, I might not be speaking the truth," Lady Newfield explained, a little hesitantly. "But from what I heard last Season, Lord Coventry was involved with a young lady. A young lady whose brother disapproved of the match as her father had been a marquess. Her brother deemed her only suitable to marry another marquess or even a duke! He did not want her to lower her rank. However, Lord Coventry would not leave her company, seemingly desperate to marry her."

Delilah clutched at her heart. "What happened?"

"It appears, according to the Marquess of Chesterton, that Lord Coventry attacked him during a dinner party that Lord Chesterton was hosting. I believe Lord Coventry was invited as a gesture of goodwill, *not* to encourage the match between himself and the lady in question." Sighing, Lady Newfield continued with a heaviness in her voice. "It happened at the very end of the evening, when all but he had taken their leave. Lord Chesterton described how Lord Coventry refused to leave and began to demand to know why he had not allowed his sister to continue to court him. When Lord Chesterton refused to acquiesce, it seems that Lord Coventry attacked him quite viciously."

Her heart began to beat in a panicked rhythm. "Are you speaking the truth?"

"This is all that I know," Lady Newfield reminded her, holding up both hands as though she wanted to defend herself in some way. "I cannot state that it is the truth, for Lord Coventry denies that it occurred as Lord Chesterton said."

"But Lord Chesterton must have had the injuries to prove it," Delilah said slowly as Lady Newfield nodded. "And I presume that his attachment to the lady came to naught."

"Indeed," Lady Newfield said, sighing. "It could not come to anything, not when he had injured her brother so badly. She is wed to a marquess now, I believe. He should never have behaved that way, of course, although I should state that he protests his innocence entirely."

Delilah tried to take in long, steadying breaths so that she would not begin to panic. She had asked Lady Newfield to tell her the truth, and thus, she had done so. It was best for her to know everything now rather than be told it the following evening when she met him at the ball."

"Some in society believe him, but on the whole, he is disgraced amongst the *ton*," Lady Newfield finished, now attempting to prepare Delilah for what her life might easily become when she married Lord Coventry. "His presence in London will surely be only to find a suitable wife, for he is required to continue his family line, of course."

"And my uncle saw a convenient opportunity to remove me from his concern and, at the same time, furnish Lord Coventry with what he desires," Delilah said dully, her spirits low. "And if Lord Coventry was desperate enough to perhaps purchase a wife, then I am certain that he would have furnished my uncle with whatever my uncle required."

Lady Newfield nodded, her expression one of sympathy. "I do not mean to upset you further, my dear," she said quietly. "But it is best, perhaps, that you know all. Although it will be entirely up to you as to whether or not you believe him to be guilty of such a crime."

"I do not think it matters what I believe," Delilah replied miserably. "I am to marry him whether he is guilty of such a thing or not."

Tilting her head, Lady Newfield regarded Delilah carefully. "You may think it will not matter," she said slowly, as though considering every word that she spoke, "but in time, you may discover that it matters a great deal to your husband."

Delilah shook her head, unable to speak such was the heavy weight on her chest. Her uncle never gave even a moment of consideration to what Delilah herself thought, so why should her husband-to-be behave any differently?

"Have some more tea," Lady Newfield said gently, rising from her chair and pouring tea into both of their cups. "And let us try not to dwell on such fears. All you need to concentrate on at present is tomorrow evening."

"The ball," Delilah reminded herself aloud. "The ball where I am to meet my future husband."

Lady Newfield smiled, although her eyes were filled with sympathy. "The ball where you shall meet your betrothed," she agreed softly. "But where you will certainly *not* be alone."

CHAPTER TWO

Timothy did not particularly want to be there this evening and, from the looks on the faces of those who surrounded him, his presence was not desired either. Steeling himself, he kept his head high and looked all around him, not shrinking away nor back. He would not allow them to think poorly of him, not when he knew for certain that he had done nothing to Lord Chesterton, no matter what the gentleman himself said.

"You look as though a thundercloud is sitting directly above your head."

Timothy grimaced and shot his friend a dark look, which Lord Holland accepted without so much as a flicker of a frown. Instead, he grinned, his countenance bright as he glanced about the room.

"They do not seem very friendly this evening, do they?" he commented as Timothy rolled his eyes at his friend's remark. "Are they pushing you away? Is that what troubles you so?"

"It does not matter to me what they think of me,"

Timothy growled, knowing that such words from his mouth were nothing more than lies. "They are fools, all of them."

Lord Holland scowled, the smile vanishing. "They are not all fools, Coventry," he said, a warning note in his voice. "They are entitled to believe Lord Chesterton if that is what they so wish."

Timothy growled, but his friend did not remove himself from his side nor retract his comment.

"You know very well that I am certain you did not attack Lord Chesterton," he continued with a wave of his hand. "I trust you when you say you did not, simply because of the friendship that we share with one another. But others do not know you as I, and thus, they believe the word of Lord Chesterton."

"The man lied," Timothy growled, his jaw working furiously as he recalled how Lord Chesterton had revealed his injuries to all the guests at a ball that Timothy had thrown. Lord Chesterton had swaggered into the room, inciting gasps of shock and dismay from everyone. Timothy had stared in horror as Lord Chesterton had garnered everyone's attention by declaring that Timothy had beaten him the night of his dinner party and that he alone was responsible for these injuries.

The reality had been that Timothy, whilst being the last to take his leave, had left Lord Chesterton uninjured and had even spoken to him briefly about his sister, the lovely Lady Margaret, whom Timothy had thought himself in love with. He had explained that whilst he understood the reasons for Lord Chesterton's decision, he was deeply disappointed and could only pray that she would find someone worthy of her—and then he had taken his leave.

Why Lord Chesterton had done such a thing to him, why he had pretended that it had been Timothy who had been the one to injure him so, Timothy had never understood. He had been made the scapegoat and even now, one year later, his reputation was still badly tainted. The disgrace that surrounded him was more than a little upsetting, for it was a disgrace that he did not deserve. Lady Parrington—as she was now—had never spoken to him again, turning from him within society and making it quite plain that she would not so much as look at him again. Even their mutual acquaintance, Lady Rachelle, had sided with society, choosing to turn her back on him entirely.

And, unfortunately, for whatever reason, this was something Timothy had to endure, regardless of whether or not he claimed his innocence in the matter. Everyone knew that he had something against Lord Chesterton and thus, the *beau monde*, almost as a whole, believed that he had done this terrible thing. It was just as well he was an earl, for most likely, had he been anything lower, the *ton* would have given him the cut and he would not have been welcome anywhere at all.

"Have you asked anyone to dance this evening, then?" Lord Holland asked, changing the conversation entirely. "Do you dare to do so?"

"I have not done so as yet," Timothy replied smartly. "But I am certain that I shall do so." He had not told Lord Holland yet about his intentions to be introduced to, to dance with, and to assess Miss Delilah Mullins, his intended. If he found himself quite pleased with her, as her uncle was certain he would, then the marriage would begin to be planned almost immediately.

"And which of the pleasing young ladies has caught your eye this evening?" Lord Holland pressed, his questions beginning to irritate Timothy somewhat. "They all look quite marvelous, indeed, I must say." His grin was a little salacious and Timothy rolled his eyes, knowing full well that Lord Holland had no intention of courting and thereafter marrying a lady of his choosing. Lord Holland merely enjoyed the company of as many beautiful young ladies as possible.

"I must confess, there is a young lady that has captured my attention, although I do not know who she is," Lord Holland continued, having either ignored Timothy's rolling of his eyes or not quite caught it. "Do you see her?" He gestured with his chin, pointing it straight ahead of him. With an inward sigh, Timothy forced himself to look at whoever this young lady was, seeing a slender young woman with nondescript brown hair pulled back into an elegant style. Her eyes were huge, seemingly a little large for her face, and she was twisting her hands in front of her in a nervous fashion. Her gown was of the highest quality, however, even if the light cream shade pulled the color from her cheeks.

"Then why do you not go and seek an introduction to her?" Timothy asked, not particularly interested in the lady. "There must be someone here who knows who she is."

Lord Holland chuckled, one eyebrow lifting. "I do

not want to make my interest *too* apparent," he said with a grin. "But yes, should I see someone dancing with her that I am already acquainted with, then I shall do everything in my power to ensure that I am given an introduction." Scanning the room, his eyes suddenly lit up. "But I see the lovely Lady Stephanie is without a dance partner at present and is speaking to Lady Arabella." He inclined his head. "Do excuse me, Coventry."

Timothy did not bid Lord Holland a farewell but simply watched his friend walk away, almost pitying the young ladies given that they would now have to endure Lord Holland's company. Lord Holland would flirt and toy with them both, asking them to dance and ensuring that he picked the very best ones remaining. But it would mean naught to him other than a mere distraction.

"Lord Coventry."

His attention was suddenly caught by the arrival of Lord Denholm, who inclined his head as Timothy looked back at him.

"Good evening, Lord Denholm," he replied, aware of the supercilious look on the gentleman's face and finding that he disliked this man immensely. Were it not for the fact that he had been given a marriage offer that he could not easily turn down, Timothy was certain that he would have had no eagerness to maintain an acquaintance with the fellow. "I presume that your niece is here this evening?"

Lord Denholm grinned, but it did not reach his eyes nor give him a kind appearance. "She is," he said, his hands held behind his back. "She is quite ready to meet you."

Timothy allowed his gaze to flick around the room. "And where is she?" he asked, making the silent point that the girl did not appear to be with her guardian. "Is she dancing?"

"No, indeed not!" Lord Denholm exclaimed as though even the thought of his niece doing such a thing was quite terrible. "She has not been permitted to dance as yet. Her godmother is with her at present."

A little surprised, Timothy held Lord Denholm's gaze. "I did not know she had a godmother."

"Indeed," Lord Denholm replied with a touch of unease. "Lady Newfield. She will be ensuring that all is well with Delilah during the Season."

Silently, Timothy wondered if this was a way for Lord Denholm to push aside some of his responsibilities by giving them to this Lady Newfield but chose not to say anything of the sort given that it would not be of any use.

"I am sure she would be glad to make your acquaintance whenever you might wish it," Lord Denholm continued, gesturing towards a young lady. "I will not press you to do so at present. At a moment of your choosing, of course." And with this, he bowed his head and stepped back, leaving Timothy staring at the young lady across the room.

It was the very same young lady that Lord Holland had pointed out only a few minutes before. She was still looking very anxious indeed, and the older lady beside her was speaking words of what Timothy believed to be reassurance. Turning back to speak to Lord Denholm, to tell the man that he was quite willing to be introduced at this very moment, Timothy was astonished to see that the gentleman had disappeared. He had merely left Timothy without explanation, clearly thinking that he would introduce himself to the lady, which was, of course, quite improper.

Frowning hard, Timothy turned his attention to the lady once more. What sort of guardian allowed such a strange introduction to occur when he was meant to be taking the greatest of care with his charge? But, then again, Timothy considered, Lord Denholm had not shown any consideration for the lady thus far, given that he had now given some of his responsibilities to the godmother. Most likely, his duty apparently complete, he had gone in search of the card room or some such thing.

Sighing, Timothy studied the lady in question, wondering just how he was meant to introduce himself without coming across as rude and improper. Even though there was a great stain about his name, he did not want to make his reputation all the worse in her eyes! That would not be a good introduction to his future wife, should she be as suitable as he hoped.

Muttering darkly to himself, Timothy looked all around for Lord Holland, wondering if his friend might be able to offer some advice, but the gentleman was nowhere to be seen. Wondering if there was someone else in the room who might know Miss Mullins or Lady Newfield, Timothy frowned hard and pondered what to do.

Then, much to his relief, he saw Lord Fitzherbert, a gentleman he was acquainted with, going to greet Lady Newfield. Without moving forward himself, he watched as Lord Fitzherbert nodded to Lady Newfield and then bowed to Miss Mullins. She executed a perfect curtsy, her eyes remaining fixed to the ground as if she were very shy or behaving with a demureness that pleased him. Lord Fitzherbert sought the lady's dance card, but she shook her head, only for Lady Newfield to take a small step closer and speak to her charge, a bright smile on her face but a firm look in her eyes. With interest, Timothy saw the young lady give the gentleman her card and, at this, he took his cue to step forward.

"Ah, Lord Fitzherbert," he said, as the gentleman took his leave of Miss Mullins. "How good to see you again."

Thankfully, Lord Fitzherbert was *not* one of the gentlemen who had turned his back entirely on Timothy and he greeted Timothy with a warm smile.

"Good to see you in society," Lord Fitzherbert said with a grin. "They have not chased you away as yet, then?"

"No," Timothy replied ruefully. "Not as yet." That would change soon, however. The moment he had ensured that Miss Mullins was just as her uncle had described, he would set a wedding date and do whatever preparations required of him before returning directly to his estate. He did not want to linger in London for long. "Might I ask if you could introduce me to the ladies you have just finished speaking with?" Turning a little more towards Lady Newfield and Miss Mullins, Timothy put a smile on his face and ignored the biting nerves in his stomach. He did not want to feel anything other than calm composure.

"But of course," Lord Fitzherbert replied, as the two

ladies turned their attention towards him—although Miss Mullins did not look him directly in the face but rather towards his left shoulder. "Might I present the Earl of Coventry?" He smiled as Timothy bowed low. "This is Lady Newfield, and her goddaughter, whom I have only just had the pleasure of being introduced to. Miss Mullins."

"Lady Newfield," Timothy said with a tight smile as he noticed the flicker in the lady's eye. Did she know who he was? "And Miss Mullins." Again, he inclined his head, seeing the way that the color began to drain from her features, leaving her a sickly pale. "Good evening."

"Good evening." Her whisper was barely audible, and Timothy's heart sank. She appeared more than timid —as though she were afraid of him and what he would do. He did not want a fearful wife. He expected his wife to have all the elegance and sophistication that would be required of a countess, meaning that she would not be able to be shy and unable to converse.

"Ah," Lord Fitzherbert interrupted before the conversation could go on. "Miss Mullins, you must allow me to take to the floor. It seems that the quadrille is about to take place!"

Miss Mullins nodded but did not smile, glancing at Timothy as though she expected him to forbid her from doing such a thing. Instead, Timothy stepped aside and spread out one hand towards the dance floor, attempting to make it quite clear that he was not about to prevent her from doing so. Tentatively, Miss Mullins took a few steps forward and Lord Fitzherbert immediately caught hold of her hand, setting it on his arm as they walked towards the dance floor.

Timothy's frown lowered all the more. This was not at all what he had expected.

"If I might, Lord Coventry," Lady Newfield said, her gaze assessing him as he looked towards her. "I will speak candidly with you for the sake of my goddaughter."

A little surprised at the lady's forthrightness, Timothy could only nod.

"Delilah—Miss Mullins—has only just come to London," Lady Newfield explained, her sharp blue eyes still searching his face as though she might be able to discover the truth of his character simply by looking at him. "And when I say that she has only arrived, I mean to say that she came to town yesterday afternoon."

It took all of Timothy's strength not to gape at the lady, astonished that Miss Mullins would be out in London after only a day. Most gentlemen and ladies took at least two days to rest themselves after what was usually an arduous journey.

"In addition," Lady Newfield continued with a small sniff of what Timothy considered to be disdain, "her uncle only informed her of the agreement between himself and you, Lord Coventry, yesterday afternoon."

This time, Timothy could not hide his shock. He stared at Lady Newfield, his mouth a little ajar as all manner of emotions slammed through him. How could he judge the lady for being too quiet and much too shy when it now appeared that she had only been aware of the arrangement since yesterday?

"She did not know of your...reputation," Lady

Newfield finished, a slight flickering frown telling him that she herself was not quite certain what or who she believed. "I had to inform her of that myself."

Timothy blew out a breath and shook his head, wishing he could step away from Lady Newfield and allow this news to wash over him so that he could take a little time to consider what to do next. "I see," he muttered, dropping his head, feeling unable to look at the lady. "Thank you for informing me, Lady Newfield."

"I do so only for my goddaughter's sake," she informed him in clipped tones. "I know that you must consider her and decide whether or not you think her suitable for you, and I would urge you, therefore, not to take your first impression of Miss Mullins to be the one you most consider."

Timothy did not immediately say what was on mind —which was that, had not Lady Newfield said something, he would have certainly had a very poor impression of Miss Mullins and would have questioned all that Lord Denholm had said. Now, at least, he could understand her shyness and what he hoped was surprise rather than fear. If she had only just been told of her engagement to him, had only just discovered the truth of his reputation, then it was more than understandable that she had behaved as she had done.

"I thank you, Lady Newfield," he said gruffly. "I am grateful for your honesty."

"Good," she said briskly as the dance came to an end and Lord Fitzherbert began to lead Miss Mullins back towards them. "Should you ever have need to ask me anything, Lord Coventry, you will find me very honest indeed."

Timothy did not respond but pushed that particular comment to the back of his mind, watching Miss Mullins intently as she came back towards them. To his surprise, she was looking up at Lord Fitzherbert intently, clearly listening to him speaking and, as they drew closer, he saw her smile. In that instant, his heart slammed into his chest as he saw her face transformed. Her eyes were bright, there was a touch of color in her cheeks, and her smile was quite wonderful. There came a sudden urge within him to make certain that he could make her smile like that also, but he pushed the feeling away almost at once. That was foolishness itself. He was there to meet his potential bride and to assess her suitability: that was all. He did not need to allow his emotions to become involved in any way, not when this was nothing more than a business arrangement that suited both himself and Lord Denholm.

"Miss Mullins," he said as Lord Fitzherbert bowed towards her, taking his leave. "I must hope you have another dance free so that I might step out with you," he said, only for Miss Mullins' eyes to flare wide, looking at something—or someone—just behind him.

"Delilah!" The voice was hard and sharp. "Did I see you dancing? I did not think that—oh! Good...good evening, Lord Coventry."

Timothy swung around and looked directly into the face of Lord Denholm. "I confess myself to be a little disappointed, Lord Denholm, if you do not intend to allow Miss Mullins to dance this evening," he said, keeping his expression grave. "Is there some reason as to why she should not?"

Lord Denholm cleared his throat and harrumphed twice, waving a hand towards his niece.

"I did not know you were inclined to dance," he said as though this was some explanation. "I would not have my niece dance if you did not."

"On the contrary," Timothy replied, shrugging. "I had only just asked your niece if she would do me the honor of dancing the next dance, whatever it may be."

Nodding fervently, Lord Denholm appeared to acquiesce without making any further complaint. Had he truly wanted to ensure that his niece did not dance for fear that Timothy himself did not dance? What else could be his reason for stating she could not do so?

"I am able to dance the country dance, Lord Coventry."

It was the first time he had heard her speak, and when he turned to look at her, he saw a fresh courage in her eyes and noted how Lady Newfield stood close to her goddaughter, her hand on the lady's arm.

"Capital," he said, and stepping forward, offered Miss Mullins his arm. She looked up into his face for a moment and he noticed that she had deep green eyes, which, he considered, were quite lovely. And then, she dropped her gaze and took his arm, and there was nothing else for him to do but lead her forward onto the dance floor, ready to dance his first dance with the lady who might one day be his wife.

CHAPTER THREE

"You will not disobey me again!"

The words her uncle had shouted at her still rang in Delilah's ears as she sat at the breakfast table. The sting to her cheek as he had slapped her, hard, had left a bruise, and Delilah had no knowledge of how to hide it. The established ladies back at the school had been cruel and much too strict, but they had never struck her across the face. There was a certain shame to being struck so and Delilah had spent most of the night crying, broken over all that had happened. Her godmother had been so very eager to have her find courage and strength but Delilah had lost the little she had the moment her uncle had struck her. She had cowered before him, tears burning in her eyes and shame weighing down her shoulders—and that feeling had not left her as yet.

Betty, of course, had been horrified to see her mistress' red cheek and tear-filled eyes. She had done all she could to make Delilah comfortable, helping her into a warm bed and pressing a cold cloth to the mark on her cheek. Delilah had said very little, keeping her stomach swirling as weakness rushed through her, which had forced her to close her eyes. That sense of weakness had not left her yet, even though it was now the following day.

The door opened behind her and Delilah startled violently, suddenly terrified that her uncle would come into the room and demand further apologies or the like for what she had done last evening. Instead, Lady Newfield was shown in by a flustered footman who did not seem to know whether or not he ought to have let her in at such an early hour.

"The master is still abed, Lady Newfield," he said as she came further into the room. "I cannot wake him."

Lady Newfield laughed and waved a hand towards the footman. "I did not come to see Lord Denholm," she said as the footman flushed with embarrassment. "Certainly, do not waken him!" Smiling at Delilah, she came to sit down beside her, only for the smile to drop from her face at once. Delilah felt heat climb into her face as she tried to look back steadily at her godmother, wishing she had found a way to cover her bruise.

"What happened?" Lady Newfield asked, her brow furrowed and her eyes beginning to burn with anger. "What did he do?"

Delilah lifted one shoulder, trying to behave as though it was not of great significance. "I should not have danced when he instructed me not to do so," she said a little hoarsely. "My uncle believes that Lord Coventry felt obliged to ask me to dance when it is well known that he does not enjoy such a thing. Therefore, I should not have stepped out with Lord Fitzherbert."

Closing her eyes, Lady Newfield let out a long, slow breath, clearly readying herself as ensuring that she was not about to lose her temper. "I should not have pushed you to do so," she said, surprising Delilah with such a statement. "I am sorry, Delilah. I did not think that your uncle would be so furious and I certainly *never* imagined that Lord Coventry would not wish to dance."

It was not something that Delilah had immediately believed, despite how fervent her uncle had been in telling her that Lord Coventry simply did not dance. She did not think that she had been the one to convince him to dance, for she had not said a word about it. He had been the one to offer to take her to the floor, but mayhap she had been wrong to dance with Lord Fitzherbert in the first place.

"I do not think that Lord Coventry felt obliged to dance with me, Lady Newfield," Delilah said, glancing at her godmother and feeling a little awkward as she spoke against her uncle. "My uncle did not want me to dance; that was the only concern he had. It was not that Lord Coventry did not wish to but rather that I had chosen to disobey him."

"Regardless," Lady Newfield said firmly, "he should not have struck you." Her eyes narrowed. "I shall make certain it does not happen again."

Delilah shook her head, fear clutching at her. "Pray, do not, Lady Newfield," she said desperately. "I should not like him to become angry with you also."

Lady Newfield's lip curled. "Have no fear, Delilah,"

she replied steadily. "He shall not dare lay a hand on either myself or you again. Now." Taking in a deep breath, she looked at Delilah again and smiled gently. "Now, are you ready for me to take you out into town today?"

Delilah's eyes widened in surprise. "Into town?"

"Yes," Lady Newfield said, her smile growing steadily. "We are to go into town and purchase you a few more new gowns."

"But I already have a new gown," Delilah replied, her heart thumping quickly as she began to panic about her uncle. "I do not think that Lord Denholm would wish to give me any more gowns or incur any more expense."

"Nonsense," Lady Newfield replied with a wave of her hand. "I shall be purchasing such things for you, not because your uncle has not the funds to do so, but rather because he might throw up something of a fuss if I had all the bills sent to him." Rising to her feet, she beckoned Delilah to do the same. "Now, ask your lady's maid to set your hair so that a curl falls over your cheek. There are cosmetics that can be applied also if that does not suffice."

Delilah found herself led away, and, within the hour, she was ready to go into town—albeit a little afraid that her uncle would suddenly appear and demand to know where she was going. Her bonnet was set just so, her hair curled and set in place. All in all, she looked quite the perfect young lady, ready to see all that London had to offer. But she felt nothing but dread.

~

"Now," Lady Newfield said as Delilah picked up a pair of silk gloves, running her fingers down over the material and struggling to believe that the large number of items ready to be purchased were all for her. "What else is it that you require?"

"I—I do not think I require anything further," Delilah replied as Lady Newfield looked down at the gloves Delilah held. "You have been very kind, Lady Newfield."

"New gloves!" Lady Newfield exclaimed, smiling beautifully as Delilah looked at her in surprise. "Of course. You must have at least two new pairs."

"Two?" Delilah gasped as Lady Newfield nodded. "I do not need more than one, surely, and I already have—"

"Delilah," Lady Newfield said, putting her hand on Delilah's arm. "You have been given very little in this life. You have had very little choice. As your godmother, it was very difficult for me not to know where you were or what had happened to you." Her smile was soft, but her eyes were glistening with tears. "Allow me now to do these small things for you. For it will not only bring you joy but it will bring me some also."

Knowing that she could not argue, that she could not refuse, Delilah only nodded, a lump forming in her throat as she saw Lady Newfield's smile grow. She then plucked the gloves from Delilah's hands and took them to the dressmaker, adding them to the list of things that she was already purchasing. Smiling to herself, Delilah moved through the shop, making certain to avoid the other ladies who had come in. She meandered slowly, taking in all the wonderful colors, the different fabrics, the beautiful items ready for someone to purchase.

"Did you see Lord Coventry last evening?"

The smile Delilah wore dropped in an instant, and she froze, her back towards the ladies that were speaking in less than quiet tones.

"I could hardly believe my eyes when I saw him dancing with that lady!" said another voice, a giggle following her words. "How dare he think of standing up on the floor in such a manner?"

"And what of the lady herself?" came a third voice. "She did not seem to think it improper for her to dance with such a disgraced gentleman."

"Perhaps she does not care about her reputation," said the first. "I should never even allow myself to *greet* him, given what the *beau monde* would think of me."

Another giggle ran through the shop, and Delilah closed her eyes, feeling heat climb up her spine and rush into her cheeks.

"The stain that would be on my reputation should I allow myself to converse with him," said the second, an affected tone in her voice, being so dramatic in her judgment upon Delilah that the other ladies giggled uproariously. "Some would give me the cut direct; I am quite sure of it!"

"Mayhap we ought to give that particular lady the cut direct," said the third, sounding considerably more haughty than before. "Does anyone know her name?"

Delilah winced and tried to make it appear as though she were looking at the items near to her but found that she could not move. A slight trembling was taking a hold of her limbs and she had to put all of her energy into remaining still.

"No," said one of the ladies, filling Delilah with relief. "No, I do not know her."

"I am sure someone will be aware of her," another said. "We shall have to discover her name at the very least, for to dance with Lord Coventry is quite foolish."

"Mayhap she does not know of his reputation," said a fifth voice that Delilah had not heard before. "There is, perhaps, a chance to show some kindness here."

This was met with a moment of silence, only for the other ladies to titter and laugh as though the suggestion were quite ridiculous. Delilah felt an urge to turn around so that she might see the fifth lady, to know whether or not she had been laughing also, realizing how foolish she had been. But she dared not say a word, dared not move for fear that she would be recognized.

"I think the lady needs nothing but a clear resolve from us not to associate with her should she continue to spend time in the company of Lord Coventry," said the first lady, haughty and determined. "There is no need nor any requirement for kindness, Miss Jamieson."

Miss Jamieson.

Delilah allowed the name to ring around her mind as she felt a small sense of relief creep over her shame, reminding her that there were, at least, a few within society who would not turn away from her with the same force and disdain as others. There might come a time where she would seek out Miss Jamieson in the hope that the lady would speak to her when no one else would.

"I do not think there is anything in here that I think I shall purchase this afternoon," said the second voice in a dismissive tone. "Shall we perhaps try Madame Russette?"

Presuming that this was the name of another dress-maker in London, let out a very long breath as she waited for the ladies to depart the shop, feeling her shoulders slowly begin to lower as the door chime rang and the ladies' voices began to fade. Slowly, she turned around—only to come face to face with a young lady.

Delilah started violently.

The young lady was looking at her with a clear gaze, her eyes fixed and steady. Her mouth was a firm line, and she did not smile. Delilah swallowed hard, lowering her gaze and murmuring a pardon before she began to turn away again.

"You are the lady who danced with Lord Coventry, are you not?"

The voice, Delilah prayed, was the one that belonged to the fifth young lady she had heard talking. Turning around, she looked at the lady again, uncertain as to what to say. If she admitted that yes, she was that particular lady, would the lady laugh in her face and mock her for being so ridiculous?

"You need not fear," the lady said, her tone a little more gentle now. "I am not about to tease you. I am sorry for what my acquaintances said."

"You—you are Miss Jamieson?" Delilah asked tenta-tively. She watched the surprise fling itself into the girl's expression, only for understanding to push it aside.

"I am," she said with a small curtsy. "You overheard my acquaintances call me so, I presume." Seeing Delilah nod, she gave a small smile, which lit up her green eyes and took some of the firmness from her expression. "Then you should know that I have no ill will towards you."

Delilah pressed her lips together, trying to keep her composure, having only just realized just how quickly her heart was pounding. "Might I ask how you recognized me?"

Miss Jamieson laughed—a light, tinkling sound that stole more of Delilah's fear. "I saw you as we came into the shop," she said by way of explanation. "However, the moment Lord Coventry was mentioned, I noticed how you stilled. Indeed, you did not move even a little during the entire conversation!" She lifted one shoulder. "I had an inkling that, even if you were *not* the lady who had danced with Lord Coventry, you were acquainted with her."

"And now my lack of denial has convinced you that I am that particular lady," Delilah finished, feeling foolish. "Yes, I will confess that I danced and conversed with Lord Coventry."

"Then I shall not judge you for it," Miss Jamieson replied with a warm smile that lifted Delilah's spirits a little. "I wanted to remain to make certain that, if you *were* that particular young lady, that you would not allow any guilt or shame to continue to linger." Her smile faded and her brows began to knit together. "My acquaintances are not particularly kind. They frequently pass judgment over those they deem to have failed in even the smallest way."

Delilah tried to smile. "You are very kind to speak to me so."

"I should not want you to feel any lingering pain," Miss Jamieson replied as though it was to be expected. "And I do not think that, for my own sake, I shall be in their company much anymore." She gestured to the door, a small yet rueful smile pulling at her lips. "Can you not see? I do not think they are even aware that I am no longer with them!"

This brought a broad smile to Delilah's lips and Miss Jamieson chuckled.

"I can imagine that you might be looking for a few new acquaintances, Miss...?" She cast Delilah a questioning look.

"Miss Mullins," Delilah said quickly, realizing they had not been properly introduced. "And I will confess the truth to you—which is that I have no acquaintances whatsoever. I am only just arrived in London."

This seemed to delight Miss Jamieson, for she beamed at Delilah as though she had given her the most wonderful news. "Excellent!" she declared firmly. "Then, I shall be your closest acquaintance in all of London, should you permit me!"

Delilah smiled—then hesitated. "I—I shall be in the company of Lord Coventry at times, however," she said, wondering if his nearness to her would push Miss Jamieson away. "I understand that you are very kind in considering me to be quite innocent when it comes to the company I choose, but he is—"

Miss Jamieson waved a hand in an impatient gesture. "I have heard about Lord Coventry, of course," she said with a frown. "I do not know what to believe, truth be told, for one gentleman says one thing whilst the other says something entirely different!" Her frown began to ease. "Therefore, I have decided to pass judgment on neither of them, unlike most in society."

"But your other acquaintances," Delilah protested, a little afraid that Miss Jamieson herself would do damage to her reputation merely by being in her company. "What will they think of you?"

Miss Jamieson considered this for a moment and then shrugged. "I think very little of their views, Miss Mullins," she declared firmly. "Therefore, I do not think I can align myself with them any longer." Her brow furrowed. "Ladies who ignore kindness and turn, instead, to spite and cruelty, are not, in fact, the sort of acquaintances I wish to have."

Delilah hesitated, feeling herself joyous at this declaration, feeling as though she might have a friend to come alongside her, yet fearing that Miss Jamieson herself might face severe consequences for befriending her.

"Please, do not look so fearful," Miss Jamieson said gently, as though she could see what Delilah was thinking. "I am quite determined to be your friend, Miss Mullins, and nothing that anyone might say shall push me from that path."

A sudden small cough had Delilah turning at once to see none other than Lady Newfield standing a little behind her, looking at Miss Jamieson with an enquiring look on her face. She was studying the lady curiously but there was no immediate sense of dislike.

"Lady Newfield," Delilah said quickly, "this is Miss Jamieson. Miss Jamieson, this is my godmother, Lady Newfield."

Lady Newfield smiled as Miss Jamieson curtsied. "How very good to meet you, Miss Jamieson," she said in a tone that was neither welcoming nor condemning. "And you are only just acquainted with my goddaughter?"

Miss Jamieson nodded. "I am," she said, a slight pink in her cheeks. "I thought to introduce myself, which I know is most improper, but—"

"You are not, then, aligning yourself with the other young ladies who left this shop only a few minutes ago," Lady Newfield interrupted, her eyes still searching Miss Jamieson's face. "I heard some things from them that I will admit to being rather displeased about."

Miss Jamieson held Lady Newfield's gaze steadily. "I can assure you that I have no interest in mocking nor injuring your goddaughter, Lady Newfield."

"Indeed, Lady Newfield, she has been offering her friendship," Delilah said hastily, praying that her godmother would not judge the lady incorrectly. "I feel quite blessed."

Lady Newfield studied Miss Jamieson for a short time and then smiled—much to Delilah's relief.

"Then I look forward to furthering my acquaintance with you, Miss Jamieson," she said, linking one hand through Delilah's. "You must excuse us now, for I must take my goddaughter away. I confess I am quite fatigued after all that has been done this afternoon!"

Delilah smiled and excused herself, feeling her heart lift just a little as Miss Jamieson smiled and promised that she would see Delilah again very soon. Leaving the shop —with many parcels promised to be delivered to Lord

Denholm's house that very afternoon—Delilah let out a long breath as she and Lady Newfield climbed back into the carriage.

"You heard what some of the other ladies were saying, I suppose," Delilah murmured as the carriage began to pull away. "Miss Jamieson was the only one who did not."

"That must bring you a little joy," Lady Newfield said, her eyes steady and her expression worried, with a furrowed brow and tightness about her mouth. "But I would advise you to be careful, Delilah."

"Careful?" Delilah repeated, not understanding. "What can you mean?"

Lady Newfield's lips twisted. "I mean to suggest that not everyone who comes to you seeking an acquaintance is true in their desire to befriend you, Delilah. Some might come to do so to mock or to tease. Some might do so to share with others what you say or do so that rumors and gossip might come all the more readily to society."

Delilah hesitated, realizing what Lady Newfield meant. "I understand, godmother."

"Then be careful and be wise," Lady Newfield said softly. "It may be that Miss Jamieson is just as she appears and that you have nothing to concern yourself with. It may be that there is nothing about her that is ambiguous and that her eagerness to acquaint herself with you is nothing other than friendship and kindness."

Delilah felt her spirits sink a little lower, the happiness that had been there only a moment or two ago already fading. "I understand, Lady Newfield."

A sympathetic smile tugged the corners of Lady

Newfield's lips. "I do not mean to upset you, Delilah, only to remind you to be careful; that is all." With a sigh, she sat back in her seat, her head resting. "Now, there is an evening assembly we are to attend today, yes?"

Delilah tried to remember, her brow a little furrowed. "Yes, Lady Newfield, I believe so."

"And if Miss Jamieson is there, then, by all means, speak to her and spend time in her company," Lady Newfield continued with a wave of her hand. "But do not express to her anything personal, anything of deep emotion that is within your heart. Not until the acquaintance has been a little more firmly established."

Delilah nodded, biting her lip and wondering if perhaps, through all of this, she had betrayed a little more foolishness than she had first realized. Was society truly as cruel and as disingenuous as Lady Newfield suggested? Or was there a chance that the beginnings of a friendship with Miss Jamieson might turn into a true and lasting friendship that would help guide Delilah through the murky waters of the Season?

CHAPTER FOUR

"Another gathering that I have been invited to merely so that I can be a spectacle for Lord and Lady Fotheringham." Timothy grimaced as he looked around the guests. Lord and Lady Fotheringham held their assembly at the great hall in London rather than at their home—and thus, there appeared to be many more guests present.

Lord Holland smiled wryly. "At least you have been invited," he replied as though that made a little difference. "Would you prefer to be sitting at home, with only your port and your books to keep you company?"

Timothy considered this, then muttered darkly under his breath. He had not wanted to attend this evening but knowing that his betrothed would be present had forced his hand. He had to, at the very least, allow Miss Mullins the opportunity to become a little better acquainted with him before he began to speak of their marriage. And given that he did not want to invite her to walk with him in a public setting as yet, he had to come to these occasions simply to be in her company for a short time.

"You would not prefer to be at home, then," Lord Holland chuckled, grinning broadly at Timothy, who disliked intensely his friend's ability to speak so openly and so frankly about the situation. "Even if you are here merely to be a source of gossip, to speak about Lady Fotheringham's ball for a few days longer, then what does it matter?"

Gritting his teeth so that he would not throw out a sharp response to his friend, Timothy closed his eyes tightly.

"You are displeased with me, I think," Lord Holland said with a heavy sigh. "I can say nothing that will please you, it seems."

"I do not like being here," Timothy replied, letting out his breath slowly. "I am only here to further my acquaintance with—"

He stopped dead, realizing that he had been about to speak of Miss Mullins but that he had not talked to Lord Holland about her as yet.

Lord Holland noticed the hesitation at once, his eyes gleaming as a broad smile settled on his face. "Indeed, you are going to have to speak of this new acquaintance to me now, Lord Coventry. You know very well that I shall not allow you even a moment's peace without speaking their name!"

Blowing out a frustrated breath, Timothy glared at his friend, but Lord Holland only looked all the more intrigued.

"I have an arrangement," he gritted out as Lord

Holland's eyes widened a fraction. "I am to find myself betrothed very soon." He waved a hand as though it did not mean anything of significance. "That is all."

Lord Holland's mouth fell open as he gaped at Timothy, who merely rolled his eyes at his friend's expression.

"Surely it cannot be that astonishing," Timothy muttered, feeling a flush creep up his face. "I am very glad that I have found someone so willing to give me their charge as my wife."

"But this is most astonishing!" Lord Holland exclaimed, only for Timothy to round on him and beg for him to keep his voice a little lower. The last thing he needed was to garner any great attention from the *beau monde* that surrounded him at present.

"You are to be engaged?" Lord Holland repeated, clapping his hand on Timothy's shoulder. "And what is the lady's name, pray tell? Does she know the truth of who she is to marry?"

Rolling his eyes, Timothy lifted one eyebrow, but Lord Holland merely grinned that ridiculous smile of his and waited.

"The lady is well aware of my reputation," Timothy lied, not telling Lord Holland that Miss Mullins had only been aware of his name and the gossip surrounding him very recently indeed. "Her name is Miss Mullins. She is the niece of Lord Denholm."

Lord Holland's mouth dropped open, and his eyes widened all the more. He said nothing for some moments but stared at Timothy as though he could not quite believe what was being said.

"You are acquainted with Miss Mullins, I think,"

Timothy continued, remembering how Lord Holland had been eager to dance with the lady. "You have been introduced to her, yes?"

Lord Holland took another moment or two to regain his speech, his eyes rounding as he continued to stare at Timothy. "Yes, I believe I am," he said slowly, his words being pulled from his mouth with a great effort as though he could barely find what to say. "I met her at the last ball we attended."

"Indeed," Timothy remarked dryly. "I recall you thinking her quite lovely if I recall correctly."

A strangled noise came from Lord Holland's lips as he shook his head, trying to clear the thoughts filling it.

"I myself have no particular feelings as yet," Timothy continued, ignoring the strange surge of protectiveness that had come over him when Lord Denholm had spoken to his niece at the ball. "I only consider whether or not she is a suitable young lady and able to be the wife of an earl."

"I—I am greatly astonished," Lord Holland muttered, his eyes now searching Timothy's face as though he expected him to be telling nothing more than falsehoods. "I did not think that you would be able to court a lady, never mind betroth yourself to her!"

A ripple of anger washed over Timothy, but he remained silent, knowing that his friend did not mean to speak so ill but that he was simply displaying his usual frankness.

"And her uncle has agreed, has he?" Lord Holland continued with wide eyes. "Have you had to pay him a great deal?"

Looking sharply at his friend, Timothy saw the gleam in his eye and knew that he could not hide the truth from him. "I have made a few arrangements, yes," he said slowly as Lord Holland nodded sagely, as if he had quite expected this to be said. "But there is nothing of great consequence. I am not at all in financial hardship due to this marriage, if that is what you are implying."

Shrugging, Lord Holland kept his eyes fixed to Timothy's. "I should not expect you to be so, given the coffers that belong to you," he said softly. "Just so long as you have not degraded yourself in any way to find a wife, Coventry. Surely a lady cannot be worth that!"

"She can if she is the only means by which I might be able to continue the family line!" Timothy retorted with a shake of his head. "You might very well be able to have such a lady within a moment or two's consideration, but I, however, find myself in a very different situation altogether." His voice was a little louder than he had intended and garnered him one or two dark looks from all about him.

Lord Holland held up both hands, looking at Timothy with a frown beginning to knit his brow.

"I did not mean to upset you," he said, keeping his voice low. "I am sorry. I did not think."

"No," Timothy grated. "You did not." Turning away, he let his breath out slowly, trying to regain his composure. Lord Holland was always ready to make light of this situation, to make what was difficult seem to be very easy indeed. He mocked and laughed when Timothy struggled and fought against the pain and the adversity that came with the false charge. For a moment, he considered if his friendship with Lord Holland was a suitable one, whether it brought him any benefits at all. Lord Holland was not an excellent friend, did not sympathize nor even attempt to understand. What use was a friend such as that?

"I think I shall fetch a little more champagne," Lord Holland said, his voice a little cold. "Do excuse me, Coventry."

Timothy closed his eyes in exasperation as Lord Holland stepped away, leaving him feeling irritated and upset. Lord Holland did not understand. How could he when he had never experienced the disgrace and the shame that came with this particular situation?

"Lord...Coventry?"

The quiet, hesitant voice told him at once who had come to greet him. Trying to push the frustration from his expression, he turned to his right and bowed. "Good evening, Miss Mullins. How very good to see you again."

She did not blush nor even smile as she curtsied, looking up at him with that same tentative gaze that had been there the first time they had met.

"Good evening," she murmured as Lady Newfield bobbed a quick curtsy. "Do you fare well this evening, Lord Coventry?"

He winced inwardly, wondering if she had witnessed any of the discussions between himself and Lord Holland. "I am a little downhearted, truth be told," he found himself saying, even though he had never had any intention of speaking the truth to her. "But your presence has helped lift my spirits already, Miss Mullins."

Again, he waited for her reaction, waited for her to

smile at him, to blink and look away in embarrassment, or even to flush just a little. Instead, she remained stoic, watching him carefully but without any evident reaction.

"There will be some dancing later," he said, feeling desperate as he struggled to know what to say next. "Perhaps you would like to step out with me?" To his embarrassment, Miss Mullins did not immediately respond. Instead, she pressed her lips together in a considered fashion, dropping her gaze. Evidently, the idea of dancing with him again was something that she felt to be embarrassing. Had there been whispers about her dancing with him at the ball?

"I think," Lady Newfield said with a gentle hand on Miss Mullins' shoulder, "that my goddaughter is a little concerned that her uncle might not approve, Lord Coventry." She smiled in a kind manner and Timothy felt his embarrassment lift just a little. "Perhaps if you speak to him about your wish to dance with Miss Mullins, he will be able to inform you as to whether or not she has permission to do so."

Timothy frowned, recalling how, at the ball, Miss Mullins had danced with Lord Fitzherbert, then with himself, and then with another gentleman a short time later. Had she been given a stern reproach from her uncle for doing so?

"I shall do so at once," he said, bowing quickly and excusing himself from them both. "I shall return the moment I have discovered the answer."

Making his way through the grand hall, Timothy kept a fair pace, moving quickly through the guests and seeking to discover where Lord Denholm might be. He could not understand why the gentleman did not want his niece to dance and feared that it might well be something to do with him. His brow furrowed as he feared the consequences that had been laid on Miss Mullins' shoulders for doing so, wanting to make quite certain that she did not face such a thing again.

"Ah, Lord Coventry!" Lord Denholm appeared to be in a very jovial mood, and it did not take long for Timothy to notice the large amount of whisky in the gentleman's glass, nor the way that Lord Denholm swayed from side to side.

"Lord Denholm," he said stiffly. "I have come to speak to you about Miss Mullins."

"Miss Mullins," Lord Denholm repeated, his eyes a little hooded. "My *dear* Delilah...has she been troubling you?" His smile began to fade.

"No, indeed not," Timothy protested quickly, holding up his hands, palms flat. "I came only to ask you if I might have your permission to dance with her this evening."

Lord Denholm chuckled, his brow furrowing. "I told her not to dance. I told her specifically that you did not care for dancing and berated her in the sternest fashion." He shook his head, sighed, and took another sip of his whisky. "But she would not listen to me, I fear. I am sorry that she forced you into taking her to the dance floor. She knows very well not to do so again."

Timothy blinked rapidly, a little surprised and irritated at the same time. "Lord Denholm, I would be happy to dance with Miss Mullins, so long I have your permission."

Lord Denholm swayed again, one side to the other. "I

do not want her making a spectacle of herself, Lord Coventry. She is only to be seen with you, is she not? Therefore, to dance with any other is shameful, surely?"

"I should not have thought so," Timothy replied, wondering at the stern manner of Lord Denholm. "I should be glad to dance with her, at the very least, whenever she should wish it."

Shrugging, Lord Denholm let out a long sigh. "Very well," he muttered with a shrug. "If you should wish to, then you have my permission, Lord Coventry."

"I thank you," Timothy replied, relieved, wondering if he could take his leave of Lord Denholm as quickly as he could. "Now, if you will—"

"You do know you have to court her now, do you not?"

Hearing the slight slur to Lord Denholm's words, Timothy sighed inwardly and let out a long breath. "I do not think there is any particular need to do so, given that she is, most likely, entirely suitable," he said slowly. "Once we have spent a few hours in each other's company, we shall—"

"Her godmother insists," Lord Denholm interrupted with a wave of his hand. "Courtship. Courtship for *Delilah's* sake, which is utterly ridiculous, but Lady Newfield will not permit me to do anything else."

Timothy frowned, seeing the frustration in Lord Denholm's expression and feeling the same irritation clasp to his own heart. "I must court the lady?"

"*Before* you become engaged," Lord Denholm said with a nod. "I am sure you understand." Not allowing Timothy to say more, Lord Denholm waved his hand again and turned around, wandering away and leaving Timothy to stand alone. His heart was beating more quickly than he had expected, finding himself both astonished and irritated that he now, apparently, was no longer simply able to declare himself betrothed to Miss Mullins but had to evidently court her for a short time! That had not been in the original agreement and, as he considered what Lord Denholm had stated, he wondered what it was that Lady Newfield had said to convince the fellow to do as she required. Lord Denholm was a hard man and yet, evidently, Lady Newfield had been able to make her demands and have them entirely fulfilled.

"Lord Coventry?"

He turned his head to see a footman waiting to speak to him. A little taken aback, he cleared his throat.

"Yes?"

"You are requested to join Lord Holland in the blue room, Lord Coventry."

Timothy frowned, looking hard at the footman. "What are you speaking of?"

The footman did not appear to be either insulted or flustered, holding Timothy's gaze. "I have had a message from Lord Holland, requesting you to come to the blue room."

"Why?"

One eyebrow lifted. "I did not ask, my lord."

Still feeling uncertain, Timothy cleared his throat again and put his hands behind his back. He was meant to speak to Miss Mullins now, to tell her that he had obtained permission from her uncle to dance with him, but this message from Lord Holland seemed important.

Given their upset only a few minutes earlier, mayhap Lord Holland had asked him to come so that he might apologize.

"Very well," he said as the footman nodded. "Where is the blue room, pray tell?"

"I shall be glad to take you there myself," the footman said, turning around and beginning to walk back the way Timothy had come at the first. Timothy followed without question, leaving the great hall and making his way through a small corridor, which then led to some other rooms.

"This room here, my lord," the footman said, bowing and then turning to depart immediately. Timothy hesitated for a moment and then stepped forward, pushing open the door handle and looking at what was, in fact, not a blue room in any way. Of Lord Holland, there was no sign.

"Holland?" he said, coming in a little closer and looking all about him, seeing the empty chairs and noting the empty fireplace. Aside from a few lit candles, there did not appear to be anyone present. Sighing, he turned on his heel—only to see what appeared to be a large, dark shadow lying on the ground in the corner. Frowning, he moved closer, only to hesitate. Something was wrong. He could feel it in his heart, and yet whatever that shape was, there was a very strong desire to discover the truth.

Leave, everything in him said. *Leave at once.*

Frowning hard, Timothy hesitated. Picking up a candlestick, he took a few steps closer, looking at the dark shape with narrowed eyes. Holding the candle out at arm's length, he caught his breath as he realized a gentleman lay on the floor, appearing to be asleep.

Lord Holland?

Swallowing hard, Timothy froze, his stomach twisting back and forth as he tried his best to come to a decision. Everything in him told him to leave this room at once, but could he merely turn his back on this man, whoever he was?

And then, he heard it. Loud, jeering voices coming closer to the room. Panicking, he placed down the candle and looked all about him, wondering if there was somewhere to hide, somewhere he could press himself without being seen by anyone.

The voices were drawing ever closer, making his heart quicken with panic. If he were discovered with a gentleman lying, seemingly unconscious, on the floor, then would those who discovered him not almost instantly assume that he had been the one to injure that fellow, given his reputation?

A large couch was at the opposite side of the room and Timothy flew to it at once, practically flinging himself over the top of it. His cravat became loose, his jacket undone, but he did not care. He knew he had to hide.

"I think he is just in here," he heard someone say just as he managed to crawl into the shadow of the couch, his breathing much heavier than he would have liked. "Shall we go in?"

A cheer met these words and the door was flung open wide. Timothy tried his best to listen to the voices, to see if he could recognize any, but none were known to him.

"I thought you said Robertson was in here?" queried the first. "Where is he?"

"I do not know," answered the second, sounding quite confused. "I was sure that he...good gracious!"

At that moment, Timothy knew that Lord Robertson —whoever he was—had been found. Squeezing his eyes closed, he tried to keep his breathing at a steady pace, too afraid to move even an inch for fear of alerting the gentlemen to his presence. It seemed quite foolish, in some respects, to be hiding from them, but if he rose now to reveal himself to them, then surely, they would wonder just what he was doing there.

"Go and fetch a footman at once," said a third voice. "He must be revived. I—"

"He has been struck!" exclaimed a fourth voice. "Look, on his head! There is matted blood."

There was a moment of weighty silence.

"I did not see it at first," said the first voice. "His hair is so very dark, and I did not imagine that he..." He cleared his throat and then his voice rang with an air of authority. "Fetch a footman at once so that we might gain all we require for Lord Robertson. And someone help me to lift him onto that couch."

Timothy closed his eyes tightly, fearing that the gentlemen would soon discover him. He lay on his side, his back to the wall, his face towards the couch and his knees drawn up to his chest. He dared not even breathe as the gentlemen lay Lord Robertson on the sofa. He could feel the vibrations of their feet on the floor as they walked, heard the couch creak as Lord Robertson's weight was set upon it.

And then, there was nothing more he could do but wait and pray that, with all the comings and goings, no one would look behind the couch, no one would see him hiding in the shadows on the floor.

Miss Mullins.

She was waiting for him to return, he remembered, wincing as he recalled just how he had promised to hurry back to her once he had gained the agreement of her uncle. No doubt she was now waiting for him, expecting him to give her news of what her uncle had said, hoping that she would be able to step out on the floor with him.

No doubt, in not returning to her, she would think all the worse of him. It would not be his impression of her that now mattered, but her impression of him—especially given that they were now meant to be courting rather than immediately becoming engaged!

"What has happened to this fellow?"

Timothy closed his eyes tightly, hearing the brusque voice of their host, Lord Fotheringham.

"I believe," he heard another voice say, the voice filled with a gravity that seemed to spread to every corner of the room, "that someone has deliberately and viciously attacked Lord Robertson. But as yet, Lord Fotheringham, we do not know who has done this terrible thing."

There came a pronounced silence and Timothy shivered involuntarily. Should he be discovered, then the blame for Lord Robertson's attack would land squarely on his shoulders. Perhaps that was precisely what had been intended.

"Then let us hope that we soon discover the culprit," Lord Fotheringham grated. "Once Lord Robertson has roused, have a footman alert me at once. I must ensure that my guest is returned home as well as he can be." There came a moment of silence. "And I do not want any of this to be mentioned to another living soul!" he declared, his voice rising just a little. "Lord Hewlett? Should there be a mention of this to anyone, should I hear a single rumor of what occurred, then I will know precisely where it came from!"

His eyes still closed, Timothy felt a shudder run down his spine. This was a very grave matter indeed.

CHAPTER FIVE

Delilah flushed as a lady glanced first at her and then at Miss Jamieson before turning her head away, making to ignore her. Her companion, however, smiled slightly as they passed, removing the threat of the cut direct.

"You should not be out walking with me, Miss Jamieson," Delilah said helplessly. "I can see that your reputation will be damaged merely by being in my company."

Miss Jamieson, however, merely laughed and linked arms with Delilah as Lady Newfield walked a little behind. "I care nothing for such a thing," she said with alacrity. "And I am quite certain that the gentleman I am to marry cares naught for such things either."

Delilah blinked rapidly, turning her head to look hard at Miss Jamieson. "You—you are engaged?" she said slowly. "I did not know."

Miss Jamieson shrugged. "We have been betrothed since infancy. I find him a very suitable match indeed, for he has an excellent title and is quite handsome. Although, I confess that his kind manner and generosity of spirit are what makes me so contented with the arrangement."

Wishing that she could say the very same, Delilah tried her best to smile. "Then I am very glad for you."

"He is back at his estate, and we will wed by summer's end," Miss Jamieson continued, with a small smile. "I am only in London to purchase all I shall need for my trousseau—and, of course, to enjoy what I can of the Season." She smiled at Delilah. "My mother and younger sister are equally pleased for the opportunity to be present, of course."

Delilah, who had met both of the ladies earlier, nodded in understanding. "Did you enjoy the evening assembly last night?"

Miss Jamieson nodded. "I did, very much," she said, looking at Delilah with a sudden curiosity in her eyes. "Lord Coventry was present also, I saw, although he did not linger for long."

Her heart twisted in her chest as Delilah looked away from her friend. "Indeed, he did not," she admitted, not wanting to speak of the pain that had lanced her heart when she had realized that Lord Coventry was not about to return.

"But I noticed that he made a particular effort to speak to you, Miss Mullins," Miss Jamieson continued with a warm smile. "Do you think he has an interest in you?"

Delilah did not know what to say. Miss Jamieson had revealed so much to her already when they were not particularly well acquainted. Did that mean that she was required to do the same?

"I think," Delilah began, as Miss Jamieson looked at her with great interest, "that yes, there is a particular interest there, Miss Jamieson. It comes from my uncle's eagerness to push me towards him."

Miss Jamieson's eyes flared. "Goodness."

"I confess that I was not aware of his reputation before this Season," Delilah said slowly. "Lord Chesterton, was it not?"

"Indeed," Miss Jamieson muttered with a shake of her head. "His sister was very much endeared towards Lord Coventry, from what I have heard. However, Lord Chesterton would not allow it. He had the lady's husband already chosen and agreed upon, despite his sister's protests."

Frowning, Delilah shook her head. "That does not seem particularly reasonable," Delilah replied softly, "but I can well understand that this is the way of things."

Miss Jamieson gave her a sympathetic smile. "Indeed," she said with a small sigh. "It is. The lady is now married and settled and all is at an end."

"And is Lord Chesterton present in London this Season?" Delilah could not help but ask. "Is his sister?"

"The Marquess and Marchioness Parrington are in London, yes," Miss Jamieson replied, with a twinkle in her eye. "And Lord Chesterton is also present, yes. I saw him at the assembly last evening."

A little surprised, Delilah lifted an eyebrow, only to realize that she did not know what Lord Chesterton looked like in any way, and thus, there was no reason for her astonishment. "I did not perhaps expect him to be at the same occasion as Lord Coventry."

Miss Jamieson let out a laugh. "I am sure that he did not expect Lord Coventry to be present!" she replied, making Delilah look at her in surprise. "Lord Coventry is in disgrace with quite a number of people within society —to the point that one might expect him to be entirely removed from all that the *beau monde* did."

"But it is not so," Lady Newfield chimed in, from behind them. "Some believe his word and trust what they knew of his character, and thus he has not been thrown from society's good graces as perhaps Lord Chesterton expected."

Delilah frowned to herself, recalling last evening's embarrassment. When Lord Coventry had not returned to take her to the dance floor, she had felt nothing more than shame and mortification, wanting to drop through the floor. Even though no one else had known of the expectation, she had felt the sting of his rebuffing for the rest of the evening. She knew nothing of Lord Coventry's character, of course, and thus could not decide whether or not he was guilty of such a crime.

"Good afternoon, Miss Jamieson."

Delilah stopped dead, only just realizing that she had fallen a few steps behind her friend as she had considered what had been said. Miss Jamieson was now being greeted by a very fine young lady indeed. There was a haughtiness in her expression that immediately pushed Delilah away, and she deliberately held herself back, not quite certain what she ought to do.

"Good afternoon, Lady Parrington," Miss Jamieson

said easily, sending a sudden chill through Delilah. "How good to see you again."

"And you," Delilah heard Lady Parrington say. "Might I also introduce my acquaintance, Lady Fenella."

Blinking rapidly, Delilah made to turn away, made to speak to her godmother so that she would not interrupt this meeting, only to hear her name mentioned by Miss Jamieson.

"I have a new acquaintance also," Miss Jamieson continued, quickly. "Might I present Miss Delilah Mullins? Niece to the Earl of Denholm."

Delilah curtsied quickly, seeing the slight curl of the lady's lip as she watched with sharp eyes as though deciding whether or not it was suitable.

"Miss Mullins, this is Lady Parrington, married to the Marquess of Parrington. And Lady Fenella." There was a slight awkwardness in Miss Jamieson's expression at the introduction, realizing that Lady Parrington had not properly introduced her acquaintance. Delilah saw Lady Fenella curtsy but look away, clearly used to having Lady Parrington garner most of the attention.

"How very good to meet you both," Delilah found herself saying before quickly introducing Lady Newfield. It came as no surprise to her that her godmother did not shy away from the Lady Parrington's supercilious expression but arched one eyebrow and looked at her steadily. Lady Parrington's tight expression lingered but she turned her eyes away from Lady Newfield as though she could not bear to look at her any longer.

Was this the lady that Lord Coventry had thought to marry? What was it about her that had drawn Lord

Coventry to her? From what she could see, it did not look as though Lady Parrington had any warmth whatsoever.

"How long have you been in town?" she asked with as much politeness as she could. "And are you enjoying the Season so far?"

Lady Parrington's expression grew pained as though she disliked the question and now found it a great ordeal to answer it. "It is satisfactory," she answered, turning her face away from Delilah. "I presume you are taking every opportunity to enjoy the Season, however." Her smile was a little twisted. "You have no need to do so, of course, Miss Jamieson, given that you are already engaged."

Delilah did not know what to say, finding the lady's condescension very rude indeed, but at the same time, finding herself intimidated by it. She looked helplessly at Lady Newfield but the lady in question was doing nothing other than glaring at Lady Parrington, her dislike very clear indeed. Lady Fenella had moved a few steps away from them all now, evidently not wishing—or knowing that she would not be permitted—to be a part of the conversation.

Taking a deep breath, Delilah tried to add something to the conversation so that she would not be as Lady Fenella was at present. "I find that London society can be rather difficult to traverse," Delilah answered after a few moments. "Although I am glad to be a part of it, of course."

"Of course," Lady Parrington remarked quickly, showing very little interest in Delilah at all and instead turning her full attention to Miss Jamieson. "I must ask you, Miss Jamieson, whether or not you have seen *him* within society."

A panic came over Delilah and she felt her heart begin to pound furiously, her stomach tighten, and a cold fear rushing over her. Lady Parrington was already condescending enough, and Delilah was a little uncertain as to whether or not she would be able to withstand any more.

Try to gain a little strength.

The silent, quiet voice within her began to grow as Miss Jamieson answered that yes, she had seen Lord Coventry—as had Miss Mullins. As she gestured to her, Lady Parrington's face was covered with evident astonishment, her eyes widening, her color pulled from her cheeks, and her mouth a little ajar.

Just whatever was the matter with the lady?

"You have seen Lord Coventry?" Lady Parrington asked as Delilah nodded. "Is that so? I did not think he was within society much at present."

Delilah's spine stiffened and she forced herself to reply with both honesty and whatever slivers of determination she could find. "He was very gentlemanly indeed," Delilah replied, her voice a little louder now. "I have danced with him once already and hope to do the same again very soon."

Lady Parrington looked at Delilah with a hardness in her eyes. "I should advise you not to do so again, Miss Mullins," she said, her lip curling again. "He is not worth your company—and certainly not your reputation."

"I am well able to make my own judgments on such matters," Delilah replied stoutly, a little astonished by her tenacity. "And thus far, I find that he is quite an amiable companion."

The harsh laugh that came from Lady Parrington shook Delilah to the core.

"My dear Miss Jamieson, how can you be acquainted with a simpleton such as this?" she cried, throwing out one hand towards Delilah. "She is to be gravely pitied indeed if she considers Lord Coventry to be a suitable companion!" The laugh continued, echoing around the park and making Delilah flush with such a heat of embarrassment that she felt as though her cheeks were beginning to burn.

"I think, Lady Parrington, that you speak rather too freely and with a little too much arrogance."

The laughter stopped almost immediately as Lady Parrington turned to face Lady Newfield, who was looking back at her with ice filling her eyes.

"Indeed, I think you should be rather ashamed of your conduct at present," Lady Newfield continued, taking Delilah's arm. "Miss Mullins, as your godmother, let me take you from this particular situation. You are to be the most elegant, the most genteel, and the most excellent of young ladies and this particular lady is not a good example of how one ought to behave." With a pointed look at Lady Parrington—whose face had now begun to turn crimson, Lady Newfield tugged Delilah in between Lady Parrington and Miss Jamieson, who was staring at Lady Newfield with wide eyes.

"Good gracious!" Delilah heard Lady Parrington exclaim as they walked away. "What sort of creature has the audacity to—"

"If you will excuse me, Lady Parrington. Good afternoon, Lady Fenella."

Within a few moments, Miss Jamieson was directly beside Delilah, her hand catching her arm.

"I can only apologize, Miss Mullins," she said breathlessly, clearly aware of the thundercloud that was in Lady Newfield's expression. "Lady Parrington was always a little conceited, I confess, but I did not ever think she would behave in such an improper and rude manner."

"It is not for you to apologize, Miss Jamieson," Lady Newfield replied before Delilah could say a word. "But Delilah, I should tell you that I thought you very courageous indeed to speak as you did."

Delilah let out a long breath, not realizing that she had been holding it for some time. "She was very rude, indeed, was she not?" she said, a little laugh escaping her. "I do hope I have not made things worse for you, Miss Jamieson."

Miss Jamieson laughed and shook her head. "I was acquainted with the lady before she wed and confess myself to have been a little surprised that Lord Coventry thought so highly of her when I knew her to be so...self-interested and proud. However, that has only increased now that she has wed." One shoulder lifted. "As I have said, I care very little for the *ton* at present and certainly do not feel any particular desire to remain acquainted with Lady Parrington." She shook her head, her brows furrowing slightly, and Delilah was certain she saw a hint of regret in her eyes. "We were rather well acquainted once but I do not think that such an acquaintance can continue, unfortunately."

Sighing, Delilah smiled and made to say something more, only to notice that the gentleman now approaching them was, in fact, the very gentleman they had been talking of only a few minutes before. Her stomach tightened almost at once, not quite certain where she was to look as Lord Coventry came closer to them, his eyes seeming to fix upon her. Whenever she glanced up at him, he was staring directly at her, his mouth a thin, grim line.

"Miss Mullins," he said, not even looking towards Lady Newfield or Miss Jamieson. "Might I speak to you?"

She swallowed hard. "Good afternoon, Lord Coventry," she said a little hesitantly as Lady Newfield nudged her gently. "Yes, I am certain that we—"

"Can it be Lord Coventry?"

The harsh, arrogant sound of Lady Parrington's voice cut through their conversation, and Delilah saw Lord Coventry startle. Slowly, his eyes turned towards the lady, his face paling as he quickly bowed.

"Good afternoon, Lady Parrington," he said, his voice low and filled with a gravity that sent a chill rushing through Delilah's frame. "I did not know you were in London."

"I have been in London for some weeks," Lady Parrington replied, not curtsying towards him as she ought. "My husband brought me here so that we might enjoy the Season together."

Lord Coventry flinched but replied quickly. "I do hope that you have an enjoyable time, Lady Parrington. There have been some wonderful occasions thus far."

Delilah watched Lady Parrington smile cruelly, her eyes glinting as she looked directly at Lord Coventry, seeming to be enjoying his tension and awkwardness. Her own hands began to curl into fists. Finding herself wishing that she could say something—anything—that might help Lord Coventry in some way.

Instead, she remained silent.

"My husband was at the evening assembly last night," Lady Parrington cooed with a wave of her hand. "You did not see him?"

Lord Coventry frowned hard, his eyes flint, his lips pulled into a taut line. His expression suddenly appeared angry, as though he suspected Lady Parrington of something but could not quite work out whether or not it was as he thought. "I did not," he said slowly, searching Lady Parrington's face. "I was otherwise engaged for the majority of the evening." He took a small step forward and Lady Parrington, Delilah was pleased to note, lost something of her arrogant smile and began to look a trifle uncertain.

"Perhaps you already knew that I was otherwise engaged, Lady Parrington," Lord Coventry continued, making Delilah frown as she tried to understand what he meant. "Were you also present last evening?"

Lady Parrington lifted her chin and looked directly up into Lord Coventry's face. "I was not," she said firmly. "Unfortunately, I had something of a headache and was forced to remain at home."

There then came a short silence as Lord Coventry watched the lady for some moments, with Lady Parrington looking up at him with a haughty expression, her eyes glinting. Delilah did not know what to say, did not know what to do, for she found the conversation to be odd indeed. What was Lord Coventry trying to do? Was there something he was trying to suggest that only Lady Parrington knew about?

"*If* you will excuse me." Lady Parrington arched one eyebrow and waited until Lord Coventry stepped aside. She looked up at him, reaching out to put one hand on his upper arm. Delilah felt something inside her twist as Lady Parrington did so, seeing the way Lord Coventry's face reddened, how his eyes seemed to lose some of their anger as he looked down into Lady Parrington's face.

She could still have an effect on him, it seemed.

"I do not think there will be much need for us to converse often, Lord Coventry," Lady Parrington murmured, her voice smooth as silk but her words biting and cruel. "In fact, there is very little reason at all for any of us to be in each other's company again." Her smile was tight, her eyes a little narrowed. "Good afternoon, Lord Coventry."

It took a moment for Lord Coventry to reply, but when he did, his voice was harsh and grating. "Good afternoon, Lady Parrington." Delilah watched his expression change yet again, his brows furrowing all the more, his eyes fastened to Lady Parrington as she walked away from them. Now he seemed confused—and perhaps, she feared, even a little upset. Was he disappointed with the meeting? Or happy that there had been a conversation with the lady he had once seemingly adored?

Lady Newfield was the first to speak.

"A somewhat unpleasant encounter, Lord Coventry?" she murmured, snapping Lord Coventry's attention back towards her and away, at last, from Lady Parrington. "Or were you glad to see her again?"

It was the very question that Delilah herself had wanted to ask. Her hands twisted together in front of her as she waited for Lord Coventry to respond, her heart beating so loudly that she feared he would be able to hear her.

"An encounter I was not expecting, Lady Newfield," Lord Coventry replied with an ease of manner that Delilah had not anticipated. "I have not seen the lady since last Season and I certainly was unaware that she was—" He stopped and gave a small shake of his head. "I was unaware that Lord and Lady Parrington were back in London."

"At least now you are prepared when it comes time to meet with Lord Parrington," Lady Newfield said practically, looking all about them as though it bored her to stand in the same place for such a length of time. "Now, Miss Jamieson, shall we continue on our walk?" She looked pointedly back at Lord Coventry. "Lord Coventry, I believe you wanted to speak to my goddaughter?" Gesturing to Delilah, she gave him a small smile. "Do not remain far from us, if you would."

For a moment, Lord Coventry appeared hesitant, making Delilah fear that he would not wish to converse with her any longer, that he would, instead, step away from her and excuse himself. Instead, however, he finally nodded and cleared his throat, holding out one arm towards Delilah with a small lift of his brow but no question on his lips. Realizing what was expected of her,

Delilah took his arm and stepped forward, seeing Lady Newfield nod in satisfaction before stepping away from them both.

It was a very awkward silence that surrounded them both as she began to walk alongside Lord Coventry. He said nothing at all, and she, for her own sake, could find nothing to comment on. She did not want to bring up Lady Parrington, and yet that was all that was on her mind. The lady had not given an excellent impression of her character and Delilah was finding it very difficult indeed to consider that Lord Coventry himself had thought so highly of the lady.

"Miss Mullins, I thought it best to speak to you after last evening," he said slowly, turning his head to look down at her. "I did not return for you when I promised that I would."

Delilah felt a flush creep into her cheeks as she nodded, daring a glance up at him. "Indeed."

Lord Coventry said nothing for a moment and when Delilah glanced up at him again, she was astonished to see a slight redness to his cheeks. Was he truly embarrassed over what he had done?

"You will not ask me why I dd not return?"

Now it was Delilah's turn to flush. "I would not even dream of it, my lord," she answered quietly. "Your business is entirely your own."

"That cannot be true, Miss Mullins, if we are to be betrothed," he said, making mention of their engagement for what Delilah thought was the very first time. "You have every right to ask me what I did and where I went.

For my promise was for you, that I would return in a moment with an answer from your uncle."

She did not know what to say, her tongue sticking to the roof of her mouth. Her uncle had never allowed her to question anything, did not expect her to remark upon anything that he had done or had chosen *not* to do. And now Lord Coventry was telling her that she had every right to do such a thing?

"You are unused to speaking in such a way," Lord Coventry murmured, clearly able to see what her difficulty was. "I quite understand, Miss Mullins. But, if we are to wed, then I shall not be contented with a quiet wife who never questions what has happened or what I have done."

"I—I do not think I can—"

"You must," he interrupted before she could finish. "I am not your uncle, Miss Mullins, and I have no intention of ever following his footsteps. I can assure you of that."

His words ignited a tiny spark of hope within her, but Delilah did not allow it to grow and burn. It was all too foreign to her as yet, too difficult for her to even imagine. To speak to Lord Coventry in such a manner, to demand to know what had occurred last evening when he had not returned for her, seemed much too improper.

And yet, that was precisely what he was asking for.

"Will you not ask me?" he said gently, making her flush all the hotter at the kindness in his voice. "Can you not bring yourself to do so?"

"I..." Her throat was dry, her stomach suddenly writhing. "I am sure whatever kept you, it was of great importance."

Lord Coventry sighed, and Delilah felt as though she had disappointed him—but to her surprise, Lord Coventry reached across with his free hand and settled it on top of hers where it rested on his arm.

"I can only apologize, Miss Mullins," he said heavily as something more began to stir in Delilah's heart. "I did not mean to leave you for the rest of the evening. Something very strange happened, and I found myself in a precarious position from which I could not move."

"I see," Delilah answered, wondering suddenly if Lady Parrington had been the reason for his delay but then recalling that she had not been present at the evening assembly.

Lord Coventry stopped suddenly, and she looked up at him, astonished to see what was now a wretched expression on his face.

"Miss Mullins," he breathed, his hand lifting from hers to pass over his eyes. "I find myself in such a state of difficulty that I do not know what it is I am to do. I fear I shall have to leave society almost immediately to ensure that I do not sink into disgrace any further, but what then of our engagement?" Dropping his hand, he shook his head, his breathing labored. "I am deeply troubled, Miss Mullins, and, truth be told, I have very few to whom I might turn. Lord Holland might well be willing to listen to me, but he does not have a seriousness of spirit and so will not be of any particular assistance."

Delilah swallowed hard, seeing what Lord Coventry required and yet feeling so entirely inadequate that she did not know what she was to do. Could she offer to listen to him? To help him with whatever difficulty that now troubled him? It would not be a particularly arduous task, but she was not confident she could be of any use. She knew nothing of society, knew nothing of the difficulties that troubled him. Besides which, she was not quite sure whether or not she knew enough of his character to see if he was speaking the truth about Lord Chesterton and all that had gone before.

"I should not have troubled you," Lord Coventry muttered, beginning to walk again so that they would not lose Lady Newfield. "Forgive me, Miss Mullins."

"Wait!"

The word pulled from her mouth before she could hold it back. Lord Coventry turned to look at her, and she saw the tiny flickering light at the edge of his eyes, recognizing that it spoke of a desperate hope that must now be in his heart. She tried to consider what it was like for him at this moment, realizing the sense of loneliness that must now fill him. Taking in a long breath, she stepped closer and looked up into his face. "I will listen to whatever it is you wish to say, Lord Coventry," she said honestly. "Without judgment or prejudice, I assure you." Her head dropped low as she realized that he might not wish for her assistance, fearful now that he thought her foolish. "That is, of course, if you think that I can be of any use to you whatsoever."

Lord Coventry let out a long breath and with a gentle finger, lifted her chin. A tremor ran through her at his touch, her chest tight and her stomach feeling as though a thousand butterflies now swirled all through her.

"You are a generous soul, Miss Mullins," he said

softly. "Yes, I should be glad to explain, even though I fear I might sound terribly odd in what I have to say."

Swallowing hard, Delilah could not bring herself to look into his eyes, confused by all that she felt, all that stormed through her, capturing her heart in a firm hold.

"I shall begin," he told her, reaching to take her hand so that he might place it on his arm. "And thereafter, I hope that you will be able to understand my absence and mayhap to forgive me for it."

Struggling to find her voice, Delilah kept her gaze fixed on the path ahead as she walked beside Lord Coventry. "I am certain I shall be able to, Lord Coventry," she said, aware of just how thin her voice sounded. "Please, tell me all."

CHAPTER SIX

Timothy saw the tentative smile on Miss Mullins' face as she looked at him and felt his heart lift. It had been a sennight now since that strange evening assembly, a sennight since he had been forced to hide for many hours until the room had been completely empty. He could still recall the stiffness and pain in his limbs as he had tried to stand up, just how loudly his heart beat as he hurried towards the door, fearful that he would be discovered at any moment.

"Lord Coventry."

He bowed quickly, smothering his surprise as Lord Chesterton drew near to him, a small smirk on his face as he watched Timothy.

"Chesterton," he grated, already despising the gentleman's company and wishing that the fellow had not chosen to come and greet him. "Good evening." He inclined his head and made to turn away, but Lord Chesterton took a small sidestep, clearly not yet ready for their conversation to end.

"You have been invited to an occasion, I see," Lord Chesterton continued, his eyes fixed to Timothy's. "How...unusual."

Timothy fought back the urge to respond with cruel words and instead merely shrugged. "I have been invited to a few social occasions," he replied honestly. Perhaps it was not as many as the year before, but he would pretend to Lord Chesterton that he was not forced to remain at home most evenings.

"It seems you have some within society who still wish to befriend you, although I cannot understand why," Lord Chesterton said dismissively. "It appears they do not know the truth of your character."

Anger began to bubble up in Timothy's chest, but he did not say a single word. He had never once laid a hand on Lord Chesterton, and yet, for whatever reason, Lord Chesterton had been the one to tell all of society that *he* had been the one to blame.

"You have seen that my sister is now married," Lord Chesterton stated with a smirk. "The Marquess of Parrington is an excellent gentleman, as I am certain you know."

"In truth, I do not know anything of his character," Timothy replied honestly. "But I am contented if she is happy and settled." Given his meeting with her earlier that day, Timothy now began to question just what it had been that had once drawn him towards Lady Parrington. She was not what he remembered, for her cruel, callous, and arrogant ways had stung his heart and his mind, making him wonder if he had ever really known her at all.

Lord Chesterton snorted. "I can assure you that she is

certainly a good deal more improved in her status than she would have been if she had been married to you, Coventry."

"No doubt," Timothy replied evenly, still battling the anger underneath his calm exterior. "Now, if you will excuse me, Lord Chesterton." He lifted one eyebrow and pinned his gaze onto Lord Chesterton's dark expression. "I do not think there is a need for us to converse further."

This appeared to anger Lord Chesterton greatly but Timothy did not care. Making his way past the gentleman, he sighed heavily as he walked through the rest of the guests, wishing that the music for the first dance would begin soon. Perhaps then he would be able to hide himself away in a corner of the ballroom, watching the other young ladies and gentlemen step out together as they began to dance. His heart was still pounding furiously, his anger still roaring to be released, but he did nothing other than clench his fists and wait desperately for the feeling to pass. He could not lose his temper now, not in the middle of a ball and certainly not with Lord Chesterton.

Perhaps that was what he intended to do, he thought to himself as a cold hand gripped his heart. *Perhaps he wanted you to lose your temper so that he could, yet again, remind society of your disgrace.*

"Oh!"

Wincing, Timothy stepped back, spinning around to look at whoever it was that had shoved him, hard. He could see no one in particular, for with all the guests around him, he had no idea which one might have done so. Frustrated, he turned back again, only to realize that he had stumbled directly into a young lady who was looking up at him with a dark frown.

"My apologies." There was no need for him to make any excuse, to tell her that someone had knocked into him hard, which, in turn, had made him fall into her. Rather, it was best merely to apologize.

"Lord Coventry," she said, making him realize that they were, it seemed, already acquainted. "If you are looking for Miss Mullins, I fear she has not yet arrived this evening."

He cleared his throat, trying to find something to say.

"Miss Jamieson," the lady continued, reminding him of her name with what appeared to be the smallest hint of exasperation. "You spoke at length with my friend earlier last week, when we took a walk through the park."

"Yes, yes," he stammered, bowing quickly, albeit rather too late. "Yes, you are quite correct, Miss Jamieson. Do forgive me for my foolishness."

She said nothing but studied him carefully, then shrugged one shoulder as though it did not matter what he had done. "You are forgiven," she said as a lady hovered nearby, clearly eager for Miss Jamieson to attend with her. "Do excuse me, Lord Coventry. My mother is eager for me to attend my sister so that she can be introduced to as many gentlemen as possible." With a twinkle in her eye, she curtsied and then excused herself, leaving Timothy to stand alone for a moment or two. Again, he glanced over his shoulder but knew that it was entirely fruitless for him even to be trying to find whoever had pushed him so hard.

It may well have been a mistake, he told himself,

setting his shoulders and making his way through the guests to a quieter spot. *Almost everyone in this ballroom is jostling each other.*

And yet still, his nerves were taut, feeling himself very wary indeed. After what had occurred at the evening assembly, Timothy was worried that someone, somewhere, was attempting to make use of the fact that he was seen as a danger and a threat.

Finding a quiet space, Timothy plucked a glass of champagne from a tray held by a footman and turned back around so that he could look across the ballroom. He had told Miss Mullins everything, half expecting her to laugh or to mock him for his foolish behavior, but instead, she had listened carefully and looked up at him with those green eyes of hers, her expression one of consideration and understanding. He had told her only of what had occurred at the evening assembly but had not spoken of Lord Chesterton, for he did not feel the need to do so.

"Lord Coventry, it appears you are hiding away this evening."

He turned quickly, his eyes taking in a vision that stood before him. For a moment, he lost his ability to speak given just how much beauty was now presented before him.

"Lady Rachelle," he finally managed to say, bowing stiffly. "Good evening." It felt like an age since he had last seen her, felt as though he had been gone for a long time to only now return to her company. "I am a little surprised that you thought to greet me this evening."

Lady Rachelle had always been a stunning young lady and had set the *ton* alight when she had first arrived in London for the Season. With black hair that gleamed and glistened with health, vibrant hazel eyes that swirled with all manner of greens and browns, an oval face, and a curvaceous figure, Lady Rachelle knew that she caught the attention of many. Including, of course, Timothy himself at one time.

"I was, perhaps, a little foolish in my decision to ignore you completely," Lady Rachelle commented, reaching out one light, delicate hand to press upon his arm. "I will not pretend that it has not been difficult to come to speak to you for fear of what damage it might do to my reputation, but I hope you can see that I have just enough courage to push myself to do so, regardless."

Timothy cleared his throat, putting his hands behind his back. "Yes, of course, Lady Rachelle," he replied, trying his best to remain entirely collected. "I can well understand your reasons for doing so."

She dropped her hand and smiled at him. "You are very forgiving, Lord Coventry."

He shrugged. "I have nothing else to do but forgive," he answered her honestly. "I have very few friends here in London already, and I certainly cannot imagine losing even more simply due to my stubbornness. Although—" He broke off for a moment, looking at Lady Rachelle's smiling face. "Although, I should warn you, Lady Rachelle, that you will not gain thanks nor appreciation from Lady Parrington if you continue with me."

Lady Rachelle tilted her head. "You are good to consider me," she answered him calmly. "But Lady Parrington is making herself something of a pariah with her loud, inappropriate remarks and her lack of proper conduct." Her lips tightened, and she looked back at him with an openness to her expression that he had not seen before. "I have found myself rather upset by some of her remarks of late, Lord Coventry. I am sure that I am not the only one."

Timothy did not know what to say, for he certainly did not want to speak poorly of Lady Parrington, especially when her once-close friend was standing directly before him. It was not that he did not trust Lady Rachelle but that he wanted to ensure there was no whisper of gossip about their conversation. He could not trust her just because she had informed him that she had no intention of drawing close to Lady Parrington any longer.

"You are remaining silent, I see," Lady Rachelle laughed, putting one hand on his arm again. "That is wise, Lord Coventry, I grant you, but I promise that I bear you no ill will."

He put his hand over hers for just a moment, a sense of relief and joy rising within him, unable to find the words to express it. When Lord Chesterton had refused to allow him to marry Lady Margaret, he had felt the entire world turn against him. When Lord Chesterton had accused him of attacking him, he had known himself lost to society and had seen the fear in Margaret's eyes the next time he had seen her. When Lady Rachelle had turned her back on him also, the world had grown all the darker. They had once been such a merry band but in an instant, everything had set itself against him.

"Thank you, Lady Rachelle," he managed to say, rather gruffly. "You are very good to speak to me again."

"I am only sorry that I have taken so long to realize

that it was foolish of me to decide against you without any true consideration," Lady Rachelle said as he let go of her hand. "You are aware that both Lady Parrington and Lord Chesterton are present this evening?"

He shook his head, his brow lowering quickly. "I was not," he said truthfully. "Thank you for informing me." He lifted one shoulder and shrugged. "In truth, I am not always invited to such occasions, so on the rare opportunity that I am declared suitable enough to attend, I must grasp it with both hands."

She nodded, the smile fading from her lips. "I am sorry you are being treated so. I must hope that, in time, the *ton* will no longer treat you as a social pariah. Perhaps my consideration of you will aid that somewhat."

"I must hope it will," he replied honestly, smiling at her. "Now, given that we are acquainted again, might I ask you how your sister fares?" He spoke of Lady Josephine, who was, in fact, keeping away from society for a time. Unfortunately, he had been the one to discover her in a most compromising position with a gentleman known to be a rogue. There had been consequences, of course, but thus far, all had been kept reasonably quiet.

"She is...suitably content," Lady Rachelle replied, her eyes shadowed. "I do not know when she will return to society. Father is quite determined that she should not return to London this year. Mayhap next year, else I fear that she will become a spinster and be nothing more than a maiden aunt."

Timothy's compassion rose, but he could not say that he was sorry for it. The lady had been foolish and she ought not to have allowed herself to have been so caught up with a rogue. The consequences were entirely on her head.

"Let us hope so," he said before gesturing to his left. "Now, let us talk of brighter things. Should you like a glass of champagne?" He snapped his fingers at the nearby footman. "I must hope that you..."

Trailing off, his eyes suddenly fixed to the figure of a young lady who was sitting close to them, shrouded in shadow. Next to her was an older lady who made no pretense of the fact that she was watching him with sharp eyes. The young lady was sitting with a very straight back, not looking either to the left or to the right but directly ahead, making it quite plain that she was not studying him.

Miss Mullins.

Had she seen him take Lady Rachelle's hand? He did not think that she had overheard his conversation, given the noise and the hubbub all around them, but even the knowledge that she had been sitting nearby and he had not even noticed her sent a flare of embarrassment up his spine and directly into his face.

"Lord Coventry?"

There was a curious note in Lady Rachelle's voice, and Timothy forced himself to turn back to her, putting a smile on his face that he did not feel. As he handed Lady Rachelle a glass of champagne and continued to inquire as to what she had been doing these last few months, Timothy tried not to notice Miss Mullins nearby. He told himself that there was no need to feel any sort of guilt or embarrassment, for he had done nothing wrong. And yet, with every word he spoke, he felt himself grow more and more twisted inside, fearful that she would think all the worse of him.

"I must excuse myself now, Lord Coventry," Lady Rachelle smiled as an older lady, whom Timothy recognized to be Lady Rachelle's companion, drew near. "I am to dance with Lord Tomlinson, I think." She glanced at the companion, who nodded but said nothing. "I must hope that one day soon, we shall be able to dance together again."

It was on the tip of his tongue to ask if she would be able to spare him a dance this evening, but for whatever reason, the presence of Miss Mullins stopped him from doing so. He was sure he caught a flicker of disappointment in Lady Rachelle's eyes as she bobbed a curtsy, his skin flaming hot as she touched his arm as she passed. Why had he not asked her? Given all that she had said, it seemed quite reasonable to expect that she would accept a dance from him, no matter what the *ton* might think! Turning around, he made to go back to her, only to see Lady Newfield rise from her chair and take a few steps towards him. He had no other choice but to allow Lady Rachelle to depart, his name not written on her dance card.

"Lady Newfield," he said as easily as he could. "Good evening."

Lady Newfield lifted her chin and glared at him. "Good evening, Lord Coventry. Are you having a pleasant evening?"

He nodded. "Yes."

"Might I remind you," Lady Newfield said with a fierceness to her voice, "that you are, at this moment, meant to be courting my goddaughter? In the last sennight, I have heard you only called upon her once to take tea! And given that there have been no social occasions that you were able to attend alongside her, I would have thought that you would have shown her a little more interest."

Timothy swallowed hard. The truth was, this last sennight, he had been caught up thinking about what had happened at the evening assembly and had entirely forgotten about courting Miss Mullins.

"Her uncle might not have a great deal of consideration for what occurs between you and Miss Mullins, but I do," Lady Newfield continued firmly. "If you wish to find yourself betrothed, as you agreed with her uncle, then might I ask you to do all you can to court her so that she does not go into this marriage not knowing anything about her husband."

A little ashamed and realizing that he had been entirely caught up with all that worried him rather than what he was meant to be doing regarding Miss Mullins, Timothy had no other choice but to speak honestly.

"I have every intention of courting Miss Mullins a little more openly," he told the lady, whose hard gaze showed she did not believe he was telling the truth. "I have not wanted to rush her into this, knowing that she only discovered the truth about our engagement recently."

Lady Newfield's eyes narrowed all the more but she stepped to one side, gesturing to where Miss Mullins still sat. "Then might I suggest that you do as you have said and go to my goddaughter, Lord Coventry."

Feeling as though he had been given a stern talking to by a person of authority, Timothy cleared his throat and made his way towards Miss Mullins.

She was not smiling and did not even glance up at him as he came to sit down beside her.

"Good evening, Miss Mullins," he said with what he hoped was a welcoming smile. "I hope you are able to dance this evening?"

Her eyes slid towards him, one eyebrow lifted. "Do you intend to go in search of my uncle again to seek his permission and use that as an excuse to remain far from me for the rest of the evening?"

He was taken aback by the sharpness of her tone, the mockery in her words. It was clear that she was angry with him, that she was deeply upset, but he had not expected her to speak so cruelly. The shock he felt must have shown on his face for Miss Mullins' went a shade of bright red and she turned her head away. He noticed how she clasped her hands tightly together in her lap, her back still ramrod straight.

Clearly, she had seen how he had behaved with Lady Rachelle.

"The lady I was speaking with was a friend of mine," he told her, wondering if this would put her at ease. "She, along with the rest of society, decided that I was not fit for their company any longer after Lord Chesterton blamed me for his injuries." One shoulder lifted in a half shrug and he could not help but smile. "It seems now that she has decided she was wrong to do so and has come to reacquaint herself with me."

Miss Mullins' expression was tight, her eyes flashing.

"I see," she said without a hint of true interest in her voice. "I do hope that you enjoyed your conversation with her."

"I did," he said, bristling. "Very much. Now." Standing up, he held out his hand. "Shall we waltz, Miss Mullins?"

He did not wait for her to respond but instead pulled at her hand as she began to rise. Within a moment, he had pushed her hand through his arm and was now marching towards the middle of the room. There were many other couples already in position and he struggled to find a space suitable for them both. Upon doing so, he bowed to Miss Mullins, expecting her to bob a curtsy, only to see the whiteness in her cheeks and the way her eyes flared wide.

Anger still burned in his chest, and as the music began, he pulled her to him, holding her in the correct position. She was stiff and unyielding but he did not care, waltzing with confidence and poise. Much to his relief, Miss Mullins was not a poor dancer but went with him without struggle, allowing him to lead her and never stumbling. And, as they continued with the dance, Timothy's anger began to fade away. Yes, he reasoned, Miss Mullins had spoken sharply, and yes, she had not acted as he had expected, but had he not treated her unfairly by not even noticing that she sat near to him? That he had grasped Lady Rachelle's hand when he knew it was something he ought not to do? Sighing heavily, Timothy looked down into Miss Mullins' face and, for the first time, noticed the fear that lingered in those green orbs.

Shame struck his heart. He had used his strength to

pull her into his arms, practically demanding that she dance with him when she might very well not wish to do so. Had he not just proved to her that he was just as unreasonable as her uncle? That he was just as cruel?

"I am sorry, Miss Mullins," he said, seeing how her eyes darted to his, her body beginning to relax a little in his arms. "I should not have pulled you up to dance. I should have waited for you to agree."

Miss Mullins pressed her lips together, turning her head away. "I am sorry also, Lord Coventry," she said, her voice barely loud enough for him to hear. "I spoke without any consideration or care. I should not have done so."

He wanted to tell her that she had nothing to concern herself with, that there was nothing for her to apologize for, but instead, he kept his mouth closed and merely nodded. The dance continued, and something more began to fill Timothy's heart. Instead of anger, there came a warmth that washed over him. The nearness of Miss Mullins to him, the way she had now relaxed in his arms, the tentative smile that tugged at her lips when he looked down at her— it all was having something of a profound effect on him.

"Everyone will be speaking of you, Miss Mullins," he said as the music came to an end. "I am sorry for it."

She shook her head and then curtsied. "There is nothing that you need apologize for," she told him, taking his arm without hesitation. "If we are to court and then become betrothed, I must become used to the *ton* speaking of me, must I not?"

It was a truth he did not like and certainly did not

appreciate. "I feel responsible for placing you in such a position."

Miss Mullins looked at him, her eyes a little wary. "I will not remove such a responsibility from you," she told him slowly. "For there is a truth in what you have said. You chose to make this agreement with my uncle, and in doing so, ensured that I would be subject to all that comes with being your betrothed."

Timothy did not know what response to give, realizing that she was correct in all she said but strongly disliking the feeling that came with it. Clearing his throat, he tried to change the subject.

"Mayhap you would like to take a turn about the gardens?" he suggested as Lady Newfield drew near them. "It is not too cold and can sometimes be refreshing after a dance."

Miss Mullins waited for a moment, seeing Lady Newfield nod, and then accepted with a murmur and nothing more. Timothy looked around him and saw the ladies whispering behind their hands or the fans that hid twitching lips. Clearly, there were many of the *ton* speaking of them, but he had to lift his head and refuse to allow such a thing to be of any importance to him whatsoever.

"Just this way," he said gruffly, gesturing to the door before them. Keeping his head held high, he walked towards the open doors, knowing that Lady Newfield was walking behind them. It was something of a relief to step out of doors, to feel the cool wind brush his cheeks. Clearing his throat, he looked down at Miss Mullins and noticed, for the first time, just how tightly she held his arm.

"I am sorry," he muttered, but Miss Mullins merely shook her head. There were other guests walking to and fro in the well-lit gardens, for there were even footmen standing with lanterns to keep the path clear.

"It is good to be outside for a time," Miss Mullins said softly. "I confess that I—"

"Lord Coventry?" A gentleman laughed hard as he knocked into Timothy, making Miss Mullins stumble. "Whatever are you doing here?"

Timothy felt his stomach tighten, anger beginning to grow within him. "I have been invited," he said firmly. "Do excuse me. I—"

"But you are out walking in the gardens with a young lady!" said the gentleman, his face a little shadowed in the darkness, meaning that Timothy was unable to recognize him easily. "That is most improper, Lord Coventry!"

Stiffening, Timothy drew himself up. "If you would excuse me," he said grimly. "My conduct is none of your concern, besides which, I think you will discover that I have a chaperone for the lady in question."

The gentleman became silent for a moment and, in that second, Timothy heard Miss Mullins gasp. Spinning around, he looked desperately for Lady Newfield, realizing that she was nowhere to be found.

"Most improper," the gentleman murmured, his voice now low and threatening, no hint of laughter in his voice. "How can you be walking with a lady without a chaperone?"

"I have a chaperone," he heard Miss Mullins say as panic began to grip him. "She must have been delayed."

The gentleman cackled. "Or mayhap *deliberately* waylaid," he said with a sneer in his voice. "I am very sorry indeed, miss, but I must find someone to accompany you to ensure your reputation is not damaged—although it is certainly stained already simply with you being present here alone with this gentleman."

Miss Mullins' hand tightened on Timothy's arm once more, and Timothy felt his rage begin to burn. "I do not know what you intend or who you are," he said, stepping forward and grasping the gentleman by the jacket. "But I shall not allow you to say anything about this particular young lady, not when we are quite correct in our conduct."

The gentleman grappled at his jacket, but Timothy held on all the more tightly, feeling his frustration burning hotter and hotter.

"Who sent you to do this?" he asked, fearing that someone had been watching him, hoping that he would step outside with a lady simply so that a situation such as this could occur. "You have been waiting and watching for me, no doubt, and I would presume that someone else has been hoping to rid us of our chaperone for a time so that we would have no other choice but to listen to whatever your demands now are."

Miss Mullins shook Timothy's arm. "Please, Lord Coventry," she said hoarsely. "Allow him free." It took a moment for Timothy to feel those words penetrate his mind but, eventually, he released his grip on the gentleman's jacket and shirt and, finally, let him go.

The gentleman was breathing heavily, stumbling backward as he ran both hands down his jacket, righting himself. Timothy glared into the darkness, not afraid of the gentleman's conduct but rather more fearful for Miss Mullins and what such a threat would mean to her.

"I have no other choice," the gentleman replied with a hoarseness to his voice that had not been there before. "The truth must come out. And you, young lady, must prepare yourself."

"There is no need for that."

Timothy could not believe his eyes as Lady Newfield marched forward, delivering a resounding slap to the gentleman before them.

"How dare you have one of your acquaintances waylay me?" she snapped, pointing one finger at the gentleman in question. "Pray, sir, what is your name?"

The man said nothing, the whites of his eyes a little more visible in the dim light.

"Do not fear," Lady Newfield continued after a moment or two of silence. "It will not be of any particular difficulty to discover it, sir. And as for attempting to ruin my goddaughter, I will make certain that your name is spoken of with contempt should you even make any such remark regarding her."

"I hardly think—" the gentleman began, but Lady Newfield cut him off at once.

"There are many things I could do and many things I could say, *sir*," she interrupted sharply. "For everyone in the *beau monde* has secrets I am certain they would wish to hide from almost everyone within society." Her voice dropped and she took a small step closer, pressing a finger into the gentleman's chest. "Is that not so, sir?"

Timothy watched in awe as the gentleman said nothing, clearly struck dumb by both the audacity of Lady Newfield and the fear that what she said would, in fact, become true. It was quite apparent that this gentleman had a number of secrets that he would wish to hide from the *ton* and Lady Newfield's threat was, evidently, something he could not expect to deal with adequately.

"I suggest, *sir,* that you go indoors again at once," Lady Newfield said, stepping aside to let the gentleman pass. "I do not think there is any need for company at present."

"I—I did not..." the gentleman began, only for him to lose his concentration and hurry forward, leaving Timothy, Lady Newfield, and Miss Mullins to stand alone together.

Lady Newfield was the first to speak, her voice low and yet filled with fervor.

"We must return *together,*" she said, emphasizing the last word. "I do not know that particular gentleman well, if at all, but I do not believe he will say anything to anyone. That being said," she continued before either Timothy or Miss Mullins could protest, "you and I shall walk in together, Delilah, and Lord Coventry, you shall follow after."

Miss Mullins nodded at once and dropped his arm, going to join Lady Newfield.

"I think a few things will need to be discussed with my godmother, Lord Coventry," Miss Mullins said quietly, her voice disappearing into the gloom. "Might you call tomorrow?"

He did not hesitate. "But of course," he answered quickly. "Tomorrow, I should be glad to call upon you, Miss Mullins." A small, quick smile caught one side her mouth, illuminated by the moonlight, and Timothy felt some of his worries begin to fade.

"I thank you," she said gently before turning to walk with Lady Newfield back into the ballroom, the picture of elegance and decorum. With a heavy sigh and one last look around the gardens, he walked in after them, his head held high but his nerves beginning to fray. Would the *ton* turn to look at him as one and demand to know what it was he had been doing with a particular young lady? Miss Mullins had enough resting on her shoulders for yet more to occur and he certainly did not want her to have to endure more than was required.

With a deep breath, Timothy stepped forward and moved back inside, feeling the enveloping sounds capture him completely. To his relief, no one turned to look and stare, no one made any remark that would bring him shame.

For the moment, it seemed, he was quite safe.

CHAPTER SEVEN

There was little doubt, Delilah realized, as she paced up and down her uncle's drawing-room. Little doubt that someone was attempting to have all of society turn away from Lord Coventry so that he would be in complete and utter disgrace. Apparently, it was not enough for them that the *beau monde* should think of him as something of a fiend; they wanted him to be gone from London entirely.

But who had cause to do such a thing?

"Delilah!"

The sharp, harsh sound of her uncle's voice had her startling violently, turning her head to see her uncle framed in the doorway, his brows lowered.

"Yes, Uncle?" she asked tentatively. "Is there something wrong?"

Lord Denholm came a little further into the room. "I have not heard of an engagement as yet, Delilah. What is it you have said to Lord Coventry that has had him refuse to do so?"

Delilah's heart slammed furiously into her chest. "I have said nothing, Uncle," she stammered, wishing desperately that Lady Newfield had already arrived. It was a lot easier to be courageous when her godmother was present. "He is to call upon me very soon and I am sure that—"

"When your godmother insisted on this ridiculous nonsense of courtship, I only agreed due to the pressure she put me under!" Lord Denholm continued, coming a little further into the room. "This ridiculous charade must end, Delilah! You will accept his proposal without further hindrance!"

"He—he has not yet proposed, Uncle," she said, only to realize that such a statement was not at all what she ought to say. Her uncle's expression grew dark with rage, his color rising and his eyes narrow slits as he drew closer to her, one hand held out and his finger pointed out towards her.

"The only reason he has not done so is because of you!" her uncle roared, making Delilah stagger back for fear that he was about to hit her. "I do not know what you have done but you have said something to him or behaved in some miserable, uncouth fashion that has *thrust* him from you! I am not at all certain now that you will even continue with the engagement!" His hand snaked out and grasped her wrist painfully. Delilah cried out with both fear and pain—and suddenly, the room was filled with another, all the more powerful voice.

"Unhand her at once!"

Lord Denholm turned around, his hand still gripping Delilah's wrist. Delilah cried out again as he pulled her with him, her eyes suddenly resting on the figure of Lord Coventry. Just behind him stood Lady Newfield, her eyes wide with shock.

"Lord Denholm!" Lord Coventry shouted again, authority in every word. "Let Miss Mullins go at once!"

Lord Denholm dropped Delilah's hand but his expression had not changed. "I think," he exclaimed, striding towards Lord Coventry, "that you will find that I am still the guardian of my niece and that, as such, I will—"

"Should I discover that you have behaved in such a manner again," Lord Coventry interrupted, not backing down from a confrontation but rather sizing Lord Denholm up without fear. "If Miss Mullins tells me that you did such a thing, if I come across a scene such as this again, then I shall make quite certain that the additional gifts I have agreed to give you thus far in exchange for your niece's hand in marriage shall not be given to you at all."

Silence enveloped the room. Delilah did not know where to look, her breathing ragged and tears burning in her eyes. Lord Coventry remained precisely where he was, glaring furiously into Lord Denholm's eyes. Her uncle remained quite silent, his lips taut and his eyes blazing with anger.

"We have already had the papers signed," he growled, sending a shudder down Delilah's spine. "You cannot—"

"I have the most excellent of solicitors," Lord Coventry interrupted, for what was now the third time.

"Do not test me on this, Lord Denholm. I can assure you that I mean every word."

With a throwaway gesture, Lord Denholm thrust out one hand to Delilah. "She requires guidance," he said as though she were not in the room. "I have not heard any comments regarding your engagement and I am certain that it is entirely to do with her behavior."

"It is not," Lord Coventry replied, striding towards Delilah and, to her astonishment, placing one hand about her waist and pulling her a little more closely to him, so that she was now entirely protected from her uncle's wrath. "It is entirely my own doing, I can assure you. But I can promise you that I have not even considered ending our agreement. The proposal will come when I believe the time is right."

Delilah could see that her uncle did not know what to say with this. Lady Newfield walked across the room to stand on Delilah's other side, and Delilah felt a single tear trickle down her cheek, her heart both filled with the pain of her uncle's demanding fury and the protection now offered by her betrothed and Lady Newfield.

"I think, Lord Denholm, that we are able to take tea without your company," Lady Newfield said, her brow furrowed and her words as sharp as daggers. "If you will excuse us."

Delilah let out a shuddering breath as her uncle lifted his chin, his jaw set, and turned to leave the room. As the door closed, her eyes clouded with tears and she could not help but break down into sobs.

"I am glad we arrived before he could do anything more," Lady Newfield remarked as Delilah tried desperately to dry her tears. "He has not done anything since..." She did not finish the sentence, but Delilah knew all too well what she meant.

"No," she answered softly as a handkerchief was pressed into her hands by Lord Coventry. "My uncle believed that the engagement ought to be almost instant, I think. The delay has quite frustrated him."

"That is not an excuse for treating you as he did," Lord Coventry grated, his hand still about her waist. "Come, Miss Mullins. Sit down."

Delilah allowed him to lead her to a couch, glad that he sat down next to her. She had never felt such comfort from him before, such protectiveness. The way he had strode across the floor, the way he had slipped his arm around her, had made her heart warm towards him, made her want to lean into him all the more. Her trust in him had suddenly burst to life, making her realize that there was nothing she need do other than allow him to protect her from her uncle's wrath.

Thankfully, her tears soon abated, and she crumpled the handkerchief into her hands, feeling embarrassed that she had displayed such a great emotion.

"I am sorry," she began to say, but Lord Coventry pressed her hand immediately, shaking his head as he did so.

"Pray, do not apologize," he said with a gentle smile into her eyes. "There was nothing you did wrong, Miss Mullins." His hand tightened on hers. "I have only one thing to ask of you."

Her eyes searched his face, seeing the kindness in the

depths, and feeling her breath catch in her chest as she held his gaze.

"I must ask you to tell me if there is ever such an incident again," he said softly. "I mean precisely what I have said, Miss Mullins. Although, of course," he added quickly as though he had been afraid that she might think the worse of him, "that does not mean that you should be afraid that our engagement will come to an end, Miss Mullins. I have no intention to do such a thing."

Delilah closed her eyes, a sudden lump coming to her throat as she heard the promise in his voice and allowed it to penetrate her heart.

"I will propose to you very soon," he promised as she opened her eyes to look at him. "But your godmother is correct. There should be a time of courtship first so that you have the opportunity to know my character and I to know yours." His lips twitched. "And so that the *ton* will not think that you have had very little agreement in such a matter, despite the fact that this is precisely what has occurred."

She nodded, not trusting her voice.

"Shall I call for tea?" Lady Newfield asked, breaking the moment between them both. "And then, mayhap, we might begin to discuss what the situation is at present with Lord Coventry." She smiled kindly at Delilah as she nodded, although Delilah knew all too well that Lady Newfield was still furious towards her uncle. Within a few minutes, the tray had been brought and Delilah had been handed a restorative cup of tea. The conversation remained fairly benign for some moments, until, finally, Lady Newfield turned towards Lord Coventry.

"Shall we speak about last evening?" she asked as Delilah nodded, setting down her teacup on the table so that she might explain all that had occurred thus far. "I was waylaid by a very strange gentleman who insisted that I was lost and must, therefore, be accompanied back inside." She frowned hard as Delilah shared a glance with Lord Coventry. "He appeared to be quite in his cups and I found myself greatly frustrated with him."

Lord Coventry's eyes twinkled for a moment. "I am surprised you did not merely bat him out of your way, as you might do a fly, Lady Newfield," he remarked, and much to Delilah's surprise, her godmother chuckled, her eyes bright.

"I did attempt to do so," she told him as Delilah listened with interest. "But unfortunately, he was a...bulky gentleman, and thus, I did not find myself able to remove him from me with ease."

Delilah shook her head. "And in the meantime, a gentleman I did not know attempted to state that Lord Coventry and I were walking together without a companion. I am well aware from Miss Jamieson that sometimes such things occur without consequence, but the gentlemen appeared to be quite determined to remove himself from us and to inform all within the ballroom that Lord Coventry had been behaving in a most improper manner."

"So someone had intended for such a thing to happen," Lady Newfield said slowly as Lord Coventry nodded. "They must have been willing to wait for the duration of the ball!"

"Both of them would have been willing to wait," Lord

Coventry commented. "They were both very determined."

Lady Newfield's lips twisted for a moment. "And you did not know that particular gentleman?" she asked Lord Coventry, who shook his head. "I confess that I did not know the other gentleman either, but it was not until afterward that I then realized that I ought to have paid his appearance a good deal more attention." Her eyes narrowed just a fraction as she studied Lord Coventry's face. "They are attempting to have you thrown from society in its entirety, yes?"

"Yes, they are. And that is not the worst of it." Lord Coventry replied, briefly telling Lady Newfield what had occurred at the evening assembly when he had been forced to hide behind a couch out of fear of being discovered. "It appears that whoever is behind this seeks to have me removed from the *ton* entirely."

Lady Newfield nodded slowly but said nothing.

"Could it be Lord Chesterton?" Delilah asked as Lord Coventry turned to her. "I know that he has stated that you attacked him in a most severe manner, clearly with the expectation that the *beau monde* would remove you from their company entirely."

"And that has not occurred," Lady Newfield added, clearly understanding what Delilah was thinking. "I am aware that society has you in a great deal of disgrace, but there are those who believe that you did *not* attack Lord Chesterton as he states."

Lord Coventry shrugged. "That may be," he said honestly. "It does appear to be the most probable, but I would have thought he might have been satisfied with the level of disgrace I have at present."

"You might well be wrong," Lady Newfield replied as Lord Coventry shrugged. "Is there anyone else that you might consider?"

There was silence for a long moment as Delilah watched Lord Coventry consider the question. Had he any more enemies? Was there more to his life at present than she knew?

"I—I cannot think of anyone," Lord Coventry said eventually. "Until last Season, my life was just as any other. I was quite contented with my lot until Lord Chesterton told me I could not marry Lady Margaret." He shrugged, his lips pulling into a wry smile although his eyes remained heavy with regret. "I did not think it possible to fall so quickly from society's good graces."

"The *ton* is a fickle friend, Lord Coventry," Lady Newfield said gently. "But, if you believe that Lord Chesterton is the only one who might have something against you, then it would be wise for us to consider him further."

Delilah looked at her godmother in surprise. What was it Lady Newfield was proposing? What precisely could they do, given that neither of them was acquainted with the gentleman?

Lord Coventry sighed and ran one hand through his hair, clearly exasperated. "I do not think there is anything that can be done thus far," he said honestly. "To query Lord Chesterton is entirely out of the question. He will not give any true answers."

Hesitating, Lady Newfield nodded slowly. "I can

make some inquiries," she said with a small smile. "An older lady of the *ton* is well able to find out almost anything!" Tilting her head, she looked at Lord Coventry steadily. "The gentleman that was injured at the evening assembly," she said slowly. "Do you know his name?"

Delilah, who remembered that Lord Coventry had already spoken of the gentleman, spoke before he could. "Was it not Lord Robertson?"

Giving her a quick smile, Lord Coventry nodded. "It was Lord Robertson."

"And are you acquainted with him?" Lady Newfield asked as Lord Coventry nodded again. "Then speak with him. Discover how he fares and what he remembers."

A thought came to Delilah's mind and she sat up a little straighter. "Might you also recall any of the gentlemen who came into the room thereafter?" she asked, a little excitedly. "Someone told them to go into that room, did they not?"

Lord Coventry was frowning, but his voice held a touch of excitement as he spoke. "Indeed," he said quickly. "And there was the footman that came to inform me that Lord Holland was within that room."

Lady Newfield waved a hand. "The footman will not give you a good deal of helpful information," she said with a frown. "He might well have thought that Lord Holland *was* waiting for you and was simply delivering a message. He would not have been able to tell if the gentleman in question was lying. But the other gentlemen who came into the room..." She looked towards Delilah and nodded. "That would be a wise idea, Lord Coventry."

Again, he nodded. "I recall Lord Fotheringham speaking to a Lord Hewlett," he answered, sending another spiral of hope into Delilah's heart. "I am not acquainted with the gentleman, but I can attempt to introduce myself to him, of course." His brows furrowed. "But it may well be that he will not accept such an introduction, however. There are those within society who reject me entirely."

Delilah drew in a long breath. "Then I shall do so," she said as both Lord Coventry and Lady Newfield looked at her sharply. Her cheeks began to burn with heat as the other two looked at her steadily, clearly surprised at all she had to say.

"I—I can do it, can I not?" she continued, a little more quietly. "I could also be introduced to Lord Robertson, if the same should happen, surely?"

"You—you could, yes," Lord Coventry replied, looking first surprised and then frowning hard as though he disliked the idea intensely. "But I think that I should be the one to—"

"If Delilah were to make the introductions, then there certainly would be less suspicion around you," Lady Newfield interrupted quickly. "Whoever it is that is attempting to throw you into such disgrace that you cannot remove yourself from it, they might well be watching you with great care to ensure that you are not attempting to discover them."

Delilah nodded quickly and ignored the nerves that were pouring through her. "I am sure I could acquaint myself with them both, Lord Coventry."

Lord Coventry hesitated for a moment or two and

then nodded, spreading his hands. "It seems I am outnumbered in this," he said, clearly a little concerned for her. "But if you believe that you can do so, Miss Mullins—which I am also certain that you are quite able —then I will admit that this particular course of action does seem to be wise."

She smiled at him in relief, only for Lord Coventry to then ask Lady Newfield if he might be permitted to spend a few minutes alone with her so that he could express what was on his mind in a more personal way. Delilah felt her heart quicken, her eyes widening as Lady Newfield nodded without even a momentary hesitation— and then turned to walk to the door. She sent Delilah a quick smile over her shoulder before she pulled the door open and stepped outside. Delilah could not imagine where she was going but knew that they only had a few minutes before she would return.

"Miss Mullins," Lord Coventry began, rising to his feet and beginning to pace up and down the room as she herself had done before they arrived. "I must speak to you in an open and honest fashion about our courtship."

Delilah's breath caught her in chest. Was he about to tell her that there was to be no further courtship? Would he propose to her at this very moment? It did not feel quite right to do so as yet, but it seemed that she was to have very little choice in the matter. She had already promised to accept, no matter when he proposed.

"The situation I am in at present, Miss Mullins, is not something that you need to consider," he continued, turning his head to look at her but making it only an occasional glance. "I am aware that I am already in a state of disgrace from the *ton* and that, unfortunately, that disgrace will rest upon you once we announce our engagement." This did not seem to please him for he shook his head and sighed once more. "Therefore, Miss Mullins, I would beg of you to consider your role in what we have discussed here."

Frowning, Delilah found it hard to understand all that Lord Coventry was trying to say. "Do you mean that you do not wish for me to find a way to secure an introduction to Lord Robertson and Lord Hewlett?" she asked slowly as Lord Coventry continued to pace. "I thought I would be able to help you."

"And I am truly grateful for your assistance," he said, turning on his heel and coming towards her, suddenly bending on his knees before her and looking directly into her face.

Delilah's heart thumped furiously, her fingers tightening together as she held them in her lap. When he was this close to her, when she was able to look into his eyes and see the different shades of brown that blended together, she did not think that she had ever seen anything more wonderful. Lord Coventry was, she had to admit, rather handsome. His dark hair, which had been neatly styled only a few minutes before, was now a little messy given the fact that he had raked his hand through it, but she found a very strange urge to do the very same as he had done. In fact, it took all of her strength not to raise her hand to his cheek, to brush it down over his skin. And from the look in his eyes, Delilah wondered if he knew precisely what she had been thinking.

"Miss Mullins," Lord Coventry continued, although

his voice was a little huskier now. "Miss Mullins, I do not want you to do anything that you would prefer not to do. This battle, this struggle, is for me alone. For you to involve yourself might only bring you mockery and disdain from the *ton*, whereas if you left me to work through it alone, then I—"

"You are to be my husband, Lord Coventry," Delilah found herself saying, her heart filling with all that she wanted to say to him. "When I first heard of what you had done to Lord Chesterton—"

"What I had *allegedly* done," he interrupted, and Delilah smiled. Unable to prevent herself, she touched his cheek with tentative fingers, wanting to remove the lines of frustration and pain from his face, and Lord Coventry jerked back in astonishment, his gaze fixed to hers. Embarrassed, Delilah dropped her hand and looked away.

"When I first heard the tale, I confess that I did not know what to believe," she continued, no longer able to look at him, such was her embarrassment. "But now I have come to believe that, with all that has happened to you, you have been telling the truth. I do not believe that you hurt Lord Chesterton. Therefore, I want to do all I can to ensure that you are not burdened with any more false disgrace."

"Miss Mullins."

Lord Coventry's tone was gentle, and she looked back at him hesitantly. He held one hand out towards her, still crouched before her, and Delilah slowly lifted her hand to his. In one swift motion, Lord Coventry took her fingers and pressed them back to his cheek with such a look of longing in his eyes that she did not know what to say or do. Her fingers began to burn as he held them there for a moment, before dropping his hand once more. Delilah felt heat burst in her chest as she looked back into his face, aware that there was something truly wonderful growing between them but being quite unable to understand what it was.

"You are much too kind of heart for someone such as me," he told her gently as she began to pull her hand away. "I should never have been so callous as to come to an agreement with your uncle without even considering you, Miss Mullins. And yet, here you are offering to help me, offering to assist in any way you can." He shook his head and closed his eyes. "I am not certain that I deserve your sweetness, Miss Mullins."

Delilah did not know what to say. It was the first time that anyone had ever spoken to her in such a way, and the tenderness in his voice sent her into a flurry.

"And in the midst of this strange situation," he continued, slowly rising to his feet and looking down at her. "I should like to court you properly, Miss Mullins."

She nodded, barely trusting her voice, such was the flurry of emotions that ran through her. "Certainly, Lord Coventry."

"Then you accept me?" he asked, a small, teasing smile lifting one side of his mouth. "In spite of all the strangeness that surrounds me? In spite of the disgrace that is mine? You will accept my offer of courtship?"

Seeing the way he smiled, Delilah nodded and blushed. "I will, Lord Coventry." Licking her lips, she forced herself to speak the truth. "Not because I am forced to accept, but because I truly wish it."

Lord Coventry swooped down, took her hand, and pressed it to his lips, searing her skin and making her burning cheeks heat all the more.

"You are quite wonderful, Miss Mullins," he told her just as the sound of footsteps came to both their ears. "I confess I am glad of your company and your willingness through all of this." Kissing the back of her hand again, he reluctantly let it go and then reached out to touch her cheek for just a moment before turning towards the door.

Lady Newfield came back in through the door, a knowing smile playing about her mouth as she looked from Lord Coventry to Delilah and back again. "Are we all settled?"

"Indeed, we are," Lord Coventry replied with a smile and a short bow. "We are to go ahead as planned." He looked back at Delilah, who could only smile tentatively, aware that there had been a good deal more in their conversation than Lord Coventry was willing to divulge. "And Miss Mullins is to stand by my side, believing that I have spoken the truth about everything." Reaching out, he settled one hand on her shoulder for just a moment. "I am very blessed, indeed, Lady Newfield."

Lady Newfield smiled warmly, her eyes fixed upon Delilah. "Indeed you are, Lord Coventry," she agreed softly. "Indeed you are."

CHAPTER EIGHT

"Good evening, Miss Mullins."

Delilah smiled and curtsied quickly, feeling a good deal more anxious than she had expected. This evening was to be her opportunity to have an introduction to one or both of the gentlemen in question. Lady Newfield had, somehow, managed to discover that both of them were invited to Lord Higginson's evening soiree, although Lord Coventry had not received any such invitation.

Lady Newfield came close to Delilah after greeting their host, looking around the room and putting a smile on her face that Delilah knew hid a good deal.

"I should not rush to seek any introduction," she said slowly, speaking quietly so that no one could overhear her. "Do not make yourself too obvious."

Delilah nodded, spying Miss Jamieson in the corner of the room. "I shall speak to Miss Jamieson, then," she murmured as Lady Newfield nodded. "We have not told her as yet what we intend."

"And I would not do so," Lady Newfield warned. "It would be prudent to ensure that only the three of us are aware of our intentions."

Delilah hesitated. "I am sure that Miss Jamieson does not think ill of Lord Coventry," she told Lady Newfield. "Indeed, she came to seek me out precisely so that she might tell me that she did not think poorly of either himself or me." She shrugged. "Besides which," she continued, a little self-consciously, "she is my friend."

Lady Newfield did not smile nor even pat Delilah's arm in sympathetic understanding as Delilah had feared she might. Instead, she gave Delilah a considered look and then nodded.

"Then the decision is yours," she said without hesitation. "If you trust Miss Jamieson, then do what you think is right. I shall not judge you either way."

Gratified, Delilah walked gracefully across the room, seeing how Miss Jamieson smiled in recognition, and excused herself from her conversation to greet her.

"Good evening, Miss Jamieson," Delilah began. "Are you enjoying the soiree thus far?"

Miss Jamieson rolled her eyes, a teasing smile on her face. "The company and conversation have been a little lacking, I confess," she said with a shake of her head, "but they are much improved now that you have arrived." Glancing around her, she leaned forward in a conspiratorial fashion. "I do hope the singing and the performances on the pianoforte this evening will lift our spirits, although given some of the young ladies that are present, I fear that it may not be as wonderful as I hope!"

Delilah laughed. "I must only pray that they do not

ask me, for then I am certain I should fall short of your expectations!"

"Nonsense!" Miss Jamieson declared, laughing. "I am certain that you play very well, indeed, Miss Mullins."

Delilah, who had been well-schooled in playing the pianoforte but who also shied away from even the thought of playing for an audience, suppressed a shudder. "I do not think that I should like to perform this evening," she answered as Miss Jamieson smiled her agreement. "There are a good many guests and the thought of all of their eyes upon me is more than I can bear!"

"Then you must seek out excellent conversation and nothing more," Miss Jamieson replied with alacrity. "Fortunately, there are more than a few present who are able to offer you such a thing."

"Indeed, I am very glad to hear it," Delilah replied, feeling a sudden anxiety twist her stomach. "Tell me, Mis Jamieson, do you know a Lord Robertson?"

Miss Jamieson looked a little surprised but then nodded. "I do, yes," she said, curiosity burning in her eyes. "He is present this evening. I should be glad to introduce you if you should wish it?"

Delilah opened her mouth to explain precisely why she wanted such a thing, only to close it again as she studied her friend. Lady Newfield was quite correct. There was not a strong friendship between herself and Miss Jamieson as yet, and mayhap it would be wise to remain quiet about her intentions at present.

"I—I had heard that he was injured recently," she said as Miss Jamieson nodded. "Some terrible accident, I believe."

"The man was found with an injured head!" Miss Jamieson exclaimed, her eyes wide with evident disbelief that Delilah had not heard this particular delight. "Someone had struck him terribly."

Delilah did her best to look quite distressed. "Goodness," she breathed, one hand pressed again her heart. "I confess a rather morose eagerness to be introduced to him so that I might hear of what happened from his own lips."

Miss Jamieson's lip curved upwards on one side. "You would not be the first to seek out such gossip," she told Delilah, her eyes twinkling just a little. "I am sure I can introduce you to him, and I am all the more certain that he will be quite determined to speak to you about what occurred. Indeed, he has been telling practically everyone within the *beau monde,* claiming that he was close to death, had he not been discovered by his friends."

"Goodness," Delilah murmured, all the more grateful now that Lord Coventry had not been discovered in the room this particular situation. "How dreadful."

"I do not think that it is entirely true, however," Miss Jamieson said with a twinkle in her eye. "He was hit on the head badly, yes, but I do not think it would have ended with his demise."

"All the same," Delilah murmured, "it does sound as though he was in a state of great pain."

Miss Jamieson made to say more, only to turn her head as she caught sight of someone she recognized. "Look," she said, her voice suddenly excited. "There is Lord Robertson now."

Delilah turned as carefully as she could, trying not to make a show of looking directly at the gentleman in question. However, there was a group of gentlemen standing clustered together, and it took a few more remarks from Miss Jamieson before she realized which one he was.

"The tall gentleman with the shock of dark hair that looks as though he has not run a comb through it in a very long time!" Miss Jamieson said, turning a little more so that she could face the gentlemen in question. "He does have a rather loud voice and no doubt he is telling all of those around him all about his ordeal."

As though he had heard her, Delilah heard a loud exclamation coming from that particular gentleman, her interest suddenly piqued. It seemed as though Lord Robertson would be more than willing to speak to her about what had occurred if she could simply become acquainted with him.

"Shall we make our way towards him?" Lady Jamieson asked, a glimmer of a smile on her face. "I am sure we will be able to hear all about what has occurred should we simply just listen."

Despite the clamoring voices of anxiety rattling around her mind and the swirling of her stomach, Delilah forced herself to remain prepared. She would be able to do what was required without too much difficulty, she told herself. All she needed to do was speak to Lord Robertson about what had occurred. There was no need for her to feel any anxiety at all. All this required was a little courage.

Taking in a deep breath, she nodded, and Miss Jamieson stepped forward at once. Delilah put a small smile on her face and what she hoped was an air of interest before walking alongside Miss Jamieson towards the group of gentlemen. It did not take long for one of the gentlemen there to step aside and greet Miss Jamieson warmly, although Delilah did not know who he was either. Very quickly, she found herself introduced to a good many gentlemen, as well as Lady Oldham, who was standing next to her husband. She tried her best not to show any particular interest in Lord Robertson, greeting him as she had done with every other in the group.

"I am sure, Miss Jamieson," Lord Robertson began before anyone could speak, "that you have heard of the dire situation that befell me only recently?"

Unable to hide her smile that came from seeing two or three gentlemen roll their eyes at this remark, Delilah saw Miss Jamieson putting on an expression of affected surprise.

"I *have* heard of it, Lord Robertson," she said, her tone very grave indeed. "Although I do not think that my friend here, Miss Mullins, has heard a single thing about it."

Lord Robertson's eyes flared wide, and he looked at Delilah, his arms spread. "Then allow me to tell you at once, Miss Mullins," he said, cutting across the middle of the group to stand directly in front of her. By turning away just a little, Delilah was able to garner a little privacy from the others who, clearly grateful that Lord Robertson was now distracted, began to speak of other things almost at once.

"Miss Mullins, I must tell you of the great tragedy that *almost* befell me only a short time ago," he began, in a most dramatic fashion. "I was at an evening assembly and I—"

"Do you speak of Lord and Lady Fotheringham's evening assembly?" Delilah asked quickly, praying that this would make Lord Robertson all the more amenable. "I was present that evening."

Lord Robertson's eyes widened and he pressed his hand to his heart. "Indeed?" he said, looking greatly shocked. "Then I am very surprised that you have not heard of what occurred, Miss Mullins. Someone struck me very hard whilst I was waiting to meet with a...a friend."

This was precisely what Delilah had wanted to hear. "A friend?" she said, hoping that she was coming across as entirely innocent. "Do you mean to say that someone struck you whilst you were within the great hall itself?"

Lord Robertson hesitated, then shook his head. "I was waiting in another, smaller room," he said slowly. "I had my back to the door and when it opened, I made to turn about, expecting to see her—expecting to see my friend." Flushing just a little, he tried to smile. Clearly, there would be no hesitation in expressing to the gentlemen of the *beau monde* the sort of lady he had been waiting for, but it would be more than a little impolite to express it to a lady of quality!

"And instead, someone struck you?" Delilah questioned as Lord Robertson nodded gravely. "Goodness, how awful. Were you badly injured?" She moved a trifle closer, hoping that he would think her very eager indeed to hear all that was being said.

This appeared to help Lord Robertson a great deal, for he nodded and leaned a little closer, as though he had to speak quietly for fear of being overheard. "I bled a great deal," he said with a shake of his head, one hand reaching up towards the back of his head as though he expected to still find blood there. "Thankfully, a surgeon was called and with a few days' rest, I made a recovery. A miraculous one, I believe, given just how badly injured I was!"

"You must have had a great many people praying for you," Delilah murmured as Lord Robertson nodded sagely. "I cannot imagine just how terrible a situation it was." She shook her head, feeling the question buzzing in her mind but as yet being unable to find the words to ask it.

"I am only glad that I am recovered now," he said with a dramatic flourish of his hand. "Although I confess that what has made it all the worse is knowing that I shall never be able to identify who did such a thing to me!"

Delilah sighed heavily and shook her head, one hand pressed lightly against her heart as though she were in some sort of great pain over what had happened to him. "That is very difficult, indeed, I am sure," she said with another heavy sigh. "You can think of no one who would wish you ill?"

"None!" Lord Robertson exclaimed dramatically. "The lady—I mean..." He sighed, then looked at her askance. "You must understand, Miss Mullins, the lady I was to meet with in that blue room was merely joining my company so that we might discuss particulars regarding her..." He clearly could not think of what to say to finish this remark and ended up flushing very red indeed, unable to even look at her.

"You need not think that I shall be in any way judgmental, Lord Robertson," Delilah said quickly, which made Lord Robertson suddenly look directly at her. "I quite understand." She smiled, and his cheeks lost some of their color.

"I am very glad you understand," he said, looking as though he was relieved indeed. Looking around as though he feared someone would overhear them, he leaned in a little closer to her. "To be truthful, Miss Mullins, when I spoke to the lady about my ordeal some days later, she did not even seem to realize that I had been expecting her."

Delilah let out a murmur of surprise, tucking away that particular piece of information and keeping it to tell Lord Coventry later. Given that he was a gentleman, he would find it a good deal easier to discover the name of this particular lady—if such a name mattered at all.

"It is quite astonishing, is it not?" Lord Robertson said as though it was somehow the lady's fault that she had not known to go to him. "I was quite disturbed by it, I can assure you."

"Might I ask," Delilah began, desperately hoping that Lord Robertson now felt comfortable enough in her company to divulge a little more information, "who it was that suggested you meet this particular lady in the blue room?" She widened her eyes innocently as he looked at her sharply. "What I mean to suggest is that they might have simply forgotten to inform the lady that you were waiting for her. After all, it was a very busy evening."

Lord Robertson frowned hard, and for a moment, Delilah was afraid that he would not tell her the truth. Perhaps he would shake his head and refuse to acknowledge the question, telling her that this was of very little importance.

Instead, he began to nod slowly, and then with all the more fervor as he looked around the room, thoughtfully.

"I believe you may be correct in your suggestion, Miss Mullins," he said eventually. "That would be quite understandable, then. The lady must simply not have told her that I was expecting her."

A streak of awareness ran through Delilah almost at once. "You mean to say that it was a lady who spoke to you, Lord Robertson?" she said as Lord Robertson looked at her, nodding as though he had expected her to already understand this. "My goodness, that is all the more astonishing! Why would she not inform her friend of your waiting for her?" Delilah did not even dare to suggest that it was most improper for a lady to do such a thing, even though she was fully aware that it would ruin a lady's reputation to meet a gentleman in such a manner.

"You are quite correct, Miss Mullins!" Lord Robertson exclaimed as though he had only just thought of such a thing. "I am truly horrified that I had not realized that before. I shall have to speak to her at once and ask if she merely forgot to inform her friend. For if there is an attachment to me there that I am not yet fully aware of, I should be quite frustrated."

"As I would well understand," Delilah replied, thinking quietly to herself that Lord Robertson was the most ridiculous fellow she had ever had the chance to meet. She did not dare ask him for the name of the lady in question, fully aware that he had deliberately kept the name from her thus far. Perhaps they would be able to find out the name another way, but she did not think that Lord Robertson would divulge anything further.

"I am sure I would be able to discover such a thing on your behalf," she tried, gently. "That is, if you wish to keep things discreet."

Lord Robertson shook his head, and for the first time, she noticed a grim line playing about his mouth. "That is kind of you to offer, Miss Mullins, but quite unnecessary," he said a little tartly. "I am able to keep control over my affairs."

"But of course," she said quickly, lowering her eyes and praying he did not think her rude. "I quite understand. I do hope you can resolve the matter quickly, Lord Robertson. It sounds very trying indeed."

This seemed to bring back the jovial, amiable expression that had been there only a few moments before for Lord Robertson nodded and smiled, reaching out for her hand—which Delilah gave him at once. Bowing over it, he murmured something about her being a wonderful lady to talk with and how glad he was to have had the opportunity to make her acquaintance—and thereafter, he departed, leaving her to return to Miss Jamieson.

"You were given the full story, I think," Miss Jamieson said with a gleam in her eye. "Was it terribly boring?"

Delilah laughed and chose not to tell Miss Jamieson what Lord Robertson had said. "It certainly was rather dull to hear him mention the same thing many times over," she said with a shake of her head. "But he was very fervent in his recounting and I did attempt to be as sympathetic as I could."

"You must have done very well, given how pleased he appeared to be when he walked away," Miss Jamieson replied, with a grin. "Now, look, we are being asked to move to the music room so that we might hear some performances." She giggled and linked arms with Delilah. "Do you think that Miss Armstrong will be asked to play?"

Delilah frowned. "Miss Armstrong?"

Miss Jamieson giggled again as Lady Newfield joined them. "Miss Armstrong is one of the worst musicians I have ever had the opportunity to hear," she told Delilah with a grin. "And yet she is always eager to play."

"Then let us hope she does not grace us with her presence this evening," Lady Newfield replied, a little grimly. "For I do not think I am at all prepared for such a thing." She smiled at Delilah as Miss Jamieson moved a little ahead of them, her eyes watchful. "Might I ask if you made any progress with Lord Robertson?"

"I did," Delilah murmured. "I believe, Lady Newfield, that the perpetrator is, in fact, a lady of the *ton*."

Lady Newfield's eyes widened, but she said nothing more for it was soon time for them to find their seats and to prepare to listen to the musical performances for the evening—amongst which, unfortunately, was the well-meaning but untalented Miss Armstrong.

CHAPTER NINE

Timothy had spent the previous evening wondering just how well Miss Mullins had fared at the soiree. Then he had spent a sleepless night trying to battle through all that he felt for the lady, realizing that his heart was beginning to become involved with her. Thereafter, he had spent the morning wandering through his townhouse, unable to settle on one specific thing and instead choosing to while away the hours until it came time to call upon Miss Mullins and to take her to St James' Park so that they might enjoy a short walk together.

Lady Newfield was to attend, too, of course.

It was with a deep sigh of relief that Timothy's carriage drew up to the great townhouse. He did not have to wait for much longer now to learn what Miss Mullins had discovered last evening—if anything at all.

"Good afternoon, my lord."

The butler opened the door and welcomed him into

the house—but Miss Mullins appeared almost at once, with Lady Newfield coming to stand behind her.

"Good afternoon, Lord Coventry," Miss Mullins said quickly, bobbing a curtsy. "What a fine day it is for our walk."

He smiled at her, thinking her something of a vision in her light green gown, which highlighted the color of her eyes all the more. A few brown curls strayed from the corners of her bonnet, and when she smiled at him, her cheeks colored just a little. "I am very glad to be here, Miss Mullins," he told her truthfully. "Shall we go?"

Lady Newfield greeted him cordially as he waited for them both to climb into the carriage, offering his hand first to one and then the other. It was with growing impatience that he climbed into the carriage and sat down, looking eagerly at Miss Mullins.

"I can see that you are keen to learn what it is that I have discovered, Lord Coventry," Miss Mullins said, her eyes twinkling. "Then I shall not make you wait any longer. I spoke to Lord Robertson at length last evening— or, rather, he spoke to me!"

"Indeed," Timothy murmured, sitting forward just a little. "And what did he speak of?"

Lady Newfield chuckled. "I believe he told everyone in the room about what had happened to him, whether they wished to hear it from him or not!"

"And whether or not they had heard it before," Miss Mullins added as Lady Newfield laughed. "I heard him speaking of his ordeal very loudly, indeed, and then he told me everything all over again, once I had been introduced to him."

Aware of how his stomach was twisting back and forth, Timothy nodded but said nothing, eager for Miss Mullins to continue.

"I did not find out everything," Miss Mullins said, a slight note of warning in her voice. "However, he did inform me—accidentally, I should say—that he had gone to the blue room to meet with a lady."

Timothy felt his mouth fall open in astonishment, and Miss Mullins could not help but laugh, her eyes sparkling.

"Indeed, I was rather shocked also, but I had to pretend that I quite understood the way of things. He did try not to tell me this, I should say, attempting to hide the truth, but managed to speak the truth twice without intention."

Chuckling, Timothy shook his head. "It seems that Lord Robertson is inclined to speak a little too openly."

"Indeed," Lady Newfield chimed in, a teasing smile on her face. "Although it is helpful for us that he did so."

Miss Mullins nodded, a slight flare of excitement now burning in her eyes. "He told me that he had been spoken to by a lady of the *ton*," she said, her voice dropping just a little, as though she needed to keep such a thing a secret. "And that she had informed him that the lady he was eager to meet would make her way to the blue room so that they might...converse or some such thing."

"I see," Timothy murmured, a spark of hope flickering in his heart. "So, we cannot say who it is specifically, however?"

"No," Miss Mullins agreed, shaking her head. "He

would not give me her name and certainly seemed quite reluctant to do so."

"That is understandable," Timothy agreed. "A gentleman does not want to give the name of a lady to another lady for fear that gossip and slander will follow after them both."

Lady Newfield nodded. "Indeed," she agreed. "Although it is good to know that we are now seeking a lady."

"Perhaps," Timothy said slowly, thinking hard. "Unless the lady in question was eager to help whoever is wishing to attack me."

"No," Lady Newfield replied, more firmly than Timothy had expected. "No, we must not continue to ask who and if and wonder if there is more than we had expected. Therefore, we ought to concentrate on this unknown lady."

"I agree," Miss Mullins said, although with a good deal less fervor. "I think to continue to question does us no favors. Therefore, we should do all we can to find out her name."

Timothy nodded slowly, realizing that if he continued with his way of thinking, he would end up winding himself in knots. "Very well. How shall we do it?"

Miss Mullins, who had clearly been considering this already, immediately gave him an answer. "You must speak to Lord Robertson," she said decisively. "He is very keen to talk, I assure you!"

"And what should I seek to discover?" Timothy asked as the carriage began to slow, nearing the park. "The name of the lady?"

"That might be a trifle too difficult," Lady Newfield suggested. "Therefore, why not seek out the name of the lady that he was to be meeting? That, I am certain, is something that Lord Robertson would be willing to give up, for it would be something of a boast, would it not?"

Timothy nodded, aware that this was, in fact, a very reasonable suggestion. "Indeed," he admitted with a wry smile. "I am not certain that he would be willing to discuss such a matter with me, for I shall have to introduce myself at the first and thereafter attempt to set up something of an acquaintance with him, but—"

A burst of laughter came from Miss Mullins, and Timothy stopped speaking almost at once, looking at the lady and finding himself quite astonished by what he saw. Her expression was bright, her eyes twinkling with laughter and her cheeks bright and rosy.

She was absolutely beautiful.

"Forgive me!" she exclaimed as Lady Newfield chuckled. "Forgive me, Lord Coventry! It is only that I do not think you have anything to worry about when it comes to Lord Robertson. He will tell you everything, whether or not you have ever met him before."

He lifted one eyebrow, his lips pulling into a grin as he was tugged into her laughter. "No?"

"No, indeed not," she smiled as the footman came and opened the carriage door. "Even if you are not introduced, I believe that Lord Robertson would tell you everything without even a momentary hesitation."

"Then I shall speak to him at my earliest opportunity," he told her before gesturing for them to climb out of the carriage.

Lady Newfield smiled at him, her eyes darting between himself and Miss Mullins. "Might I suggest, Lord Coventry," she began with a knowing smile on her lips, "that you walk with Miss Mullins for a time *without* my company? I shall, of course, remain a little behind."

There was not even a momentary hesitation. "I should like that very much, Lady Newfield." Turning to Miss Mullins, he looked at her and saw her shy smile. His heart warmed. "Miss Mullins?"

"I—I should like that also," she said, not quite managing to look at him before accepting his arm. They began to walk together along the path, and whilst Timothy was fully aware that there were others walking on the path also, some turning to look at them, he did not give them even a momentary glance. His entire attention was fixed on Miss Mullins.

They walked in silence for a short time, not speaking even a word. There was a comfortableness in their silence, a joy about being simply in one another's company without the need to fill the quiet with words or noise. When his mind was not fixed on the attack upon his character, the attempts to have him blamed for something he had not done, he realized just how much he had come to care about this lady, even though they had not been long acquainted.

"You have increased in confidence, Miss Mullins," he said, his eyes looking down at her, the breeze lifting one her curls for just a moment. "The way you offered to speak to Lord Robertson was courageous enough, but now that you have done so, I can see that you are thoroughly uplifted."

Miss Mullins' smile was gentle. "I confess that I have found myself to be rather brighter in spirits since I spoke to Lord Robertson," she said quietly as though she could not quite believe it herself. "When I left the school, I had no confidence in myself whatsoever. When I suggested to Betty...she is now my lady's maid—that she come with me and leave the school altogether, that was the very first time that I had suggested something so daring." She shook her head as though she could not quite believe that she had done so. "Betty took a great risk and yet she did come with me. I found a way to be brave even though I was terrified of what would occur." Her smile faded, her eyes darkening for a moment. "But I have not been able to keep that bravery with me when it comes to my uncle."

Timothy's anger burst to life in a moment. "Your uncle is not the sort of gentleman that should be responsible for anyone," he said. "The way he has treated you is appalling, Miss Mullins." Closing his eyes, he turned to her suddenly, taking her hands in his and looking into her eyes. "Miss Mullins, the more I consider things, the more I realize that it was foolish of me to ever agree to a marriage between us without even thinking of you." Shaking his head, he winced at the harsh reality that he was left with. "I wanted to marry so that the heir could be produced, nothing more. With the scandal and disgrace following me, I knew that it would be difficult for me to find a suitable wife." Pressing her hand, he looked into her eyes. "I did not even think of what a burden the situation might be for you."

"And yet," she replied, her voice husky, "I think that now, I do not find our circumstances to be burdensome in any way."

Rather surprised, he looked into her face and tried to understand what she meant. He wanted her to express a little more but could not find the words to ask her.

"Lord Coventry, what I am trying to say is that you do not need to feel in any way guilty for this any longer. I think that we have a good understanding together. You know now that I trust your character is entirely respectable. I believe that you are a most excellent gentleman and, given how you defended me from my uncle, I trust that you will never hurt me in any way."

"Never," he vowed, his voice low and determined. "I shall do all I can to care for you, Miss Mullins. You shall lack for nothing."

The way she smiled at him made his heart pound with such a fury that he was afraid she could hear it. Holding her hands together for a little longer, he nodded, turned, and began to walk again.

"Good gracious, Lord Coventry!"

A teasing voice met his ears, and he looked directly ahead of him, horrified to see Lord and Lady Parrington walking directly towards them.

"Indeed, can it be that you are out walking in the middle of London as though you are a well-respected gentleman?"

The teasing note became cruel, the mockery unabated. "And with a young lady as well! Goodness me, Lord Coventry! Do you not know what damage you will do to this lady's reputation if you walk with her in full view of the *beau monde*?"

Miss Mullins' hand tightened on his arm, and Timothy had to force himself to remain calm, refusing to speak until he was able to compose himself. "Good afternoon, Lord Parrington, Lady Parrington," he said, his voice low. "Yes, we are out walking together on what is a very fine afternoon, as you are." Clearing his throat, he attempted to sidestep Lord Parrington. "If you will excuse us."

Lady Parrington laughed. "You are not about to speak to us?" she asked, reaching across and settling one hand on Miss Mullins' arm. "Why do you not do so?"

He did not know what to say, feeling his lips stick to each other.

"We only have a short time, Lady Parrington," Miss Mullins answered after a short silence. "That is all. And it is a very fine afternoon, one we are simply attempting to enjoy."

This, however, was entirely ignored by Lady Parrington, who looked straight through Miss Mullins as though she did not exist. Her lip curled, her eyes narrowed, and Timothy felt his blood begin to boil. There was nothing for him to say, nothing for him to do other than to excuse himself again and remove himself and Miss Mullins away from this particular conversation.

"Indeed," he said, keeping his voice low and determined. "Miss Mullins is quite correct. We should continue and—"

"You do know, young lady, that this is Lord Coventry!" Lady Parrington cried, looking at Miss Mullins with an expression of haughtiness, as though she ruled and Miss Mullins was one of her subjects. "Whatever are you doing out walking with him? You shall have no other gentlemen looking at you, eager to court you, if you are seen with Lord Coventry!"

Timothy felt heat climb into his face and his muscles tense, his breathing rapid and hurried. Words of fury began to burn on his lips, but before he could say a thing, Miss Mullins took in a deep breath and stepped forward.

"You are quite mistaken, Lady Parrington." Her voice was low, and her words unhurried, her eyes fixed to Lady Parrington's. "I have chosen to be beside Lord Coventry."

Lady Parrington laughed hard, throwing her head back and garnering the attention of some others behind and around them. "You foolish, foolish child!" she cried as Miss Mullins' cheeks filled with color. "You shall never have a chance at a suitable match if you remain here."

"Perhaps I do not need it," Miss Mullins replied steadily, although Timothy noticed how her hands curled into fists as she spoke. "As I have said, Lady Parrington, I have chosen to remain here, chosen to be by Lord Coventry's side, and chosen to stay here with him even now." Then, to Timothy's astonishment, she took a step back and linked arms with him once more, her head held high, her chin lifted, and such a strength in her voice that Timothy felt himself almost in awe of her. "I do not need your warnings, Lady Parrington. I am able to make my decisions entirely on my own."

Timothy did not know what Lady Parrington was thinking, but her eyes were fury itself. They were narrowed, her brows furrowed and her lips curled into a sneer. It was no longer Miss Mullins' hands that were tightly clenched, but Lady Parrington's. Taking a step towards Miss Mullins, her voice was shaking and furious as she spoke.

"How dare you speak to me in such a manner?" she hissed, one finger pointed towards Miss Mullins. "Do you have any understanding of who I am?"

Miss Mullins lifted her chin. "I do not think that your name or title has any bearing on this matter, Lady Parrington," she answered, astonishing Timothy all the more. "You have made your choice of husband, and I shall make mine."

At that moment, Timothy felt his stomach drop to the floor, turning to look at Miss Mullins and wondering if she realized what she had said. Then, he turned to look at Lady Parrington, seeing how she stepped backward, almost staggering as she did so. Her husband, who had said nothing up until this point, reached out to catch his wife's arm, but Lady Parrington shoved him away hard, shaking him off as though he were nothing more than an annoying fly.

"You are engaged?" she hissed as Timothy noticed the others nearby pressing their hands to their mouths in shock, making no pretense that they were not listening. "Engaged to...to *him?*"

Miss Mullins tightened her hand on his arm. "Yes. We are engaged."

Lady Parrington clearly did not know what to say, her mouth a little slack as she stared at Timothy. He cleared his throat and put his hand on Miss Mullins' as it rested on his arm. "It is quite true, Lady Parrington, I am pleased to say," he answered, feeling his lips curl into a smile despite the strangeness of the situation. "And I could not be happier."

"Nor could I," Miss Mullins agreed. "And now, if you will excuse us, we really must continue our walk."

Before he could say anything more, she had begun to move away, and he went with her, falling into step almost at once. The urge to look over his shoulder was tremendous, but he resisted it with every part of his being, knowing that nothing good would come from looking.

"She is staring after you if that is what you want to know."

Lady Newfield came to join them as they walked, her face a little flushed but her eyes bright. "I do not think she knew what to say, Lord Coventry!"

"Which is unlike her," he mumbled, suddenly realizing that the Lady Parrington he now knew was nothing like the Lady Margaret he had once convinced himself to be in love with. "I must say, I am astonished at her cruel and vile words."

"Are you?" Miss Mullins replied, looking up at him, clearly a little surprised. "When I first spoke to her, I found her very much the same as she was just now, if not a little quieter."

Timothy's brow furrowed and he bit his lip. When he had looked into Lady Parrington's face, he had found that he felt nothing at all. There was no hint of the love he had once had, the joy that had come with simply being in her company. He had felt nothing for her whatsoever.

"And you did remarkably well, my dear!"

Lady Newfield was smiling at Miss Mullins, who was

smiling self-consciously. "I found a new sense of bravery, I think."

"You certainly did!" Lady Newfield cried as Timothy beamed at Miss Mullins. "You came to your betrothed's defense and showed valor that I think even a knight of old would be proud of."

They walked in silence for a short time until, finally, Timothy felt Miss Mullins gently tug his arm.

"Lord Coventry?"

Glancing down at Miss Mullins, he took in her red cheeks and the question in her eyes.

"I—I did not do wrong, did I?"

"Good gracious, no!" He stopped in an instant, holding Miss Mullins' hands in his and ignoring Lady Newfield completely. "I am more than contented to be engaged to you—if that is what you wish?"

Her smile spread across her face beautifully, her eyes lit up with fresh hope, a new joy. "Yes," she replied softly. "Yes, Lord Coventry. That is exactly what I wish."

"Then it is done," he answered, wishing that they were not in the company of Lady Newfield so that he might pull her close. "We are engaged, Miss Mullins. I shall one day be your husband."

"And I your wife," she answered, leaning a little closer. "I can hardly believe it."

"Nor I!" Lady Newfield answered briskly, coming towards them both and interrupting the conversation. "Now, shall we continue our walk? From the shrieking behind us, I believe that we have left Lady Parrington in a state of deep frustration."

Timothy had not noticed the loud exclamations until

now, but turning his head, he saw Lord Parrington attempting to pull Lady Parrington away from where the crowd of onlookers currently watched.

"Is it not interesting?" Miss Mullins murmured as they began to walk again, a little more quickly.

"What caught your interest?" he asked, feeling his heart fill with gladness as he realized he now walked alongside his betrothed. "Something to do with Lady Parrington?"

"Indeed," she answered, her hands tight on his arm. "Lady Parrington spoke a great deal, did she not?"

Lady Newfield nodded. "She did."

"But Lord Parrington said not a word," Miss Mullins mused quietly. "In fact, when he attempted to help her, she cast him aside, did she not?"

"That is true," he agreed, beginning to question everything he had once known about Lady Parrington. "A good observation, Miss Mullins."

"One that would be worth considering further," Lady Newfield said before they began to slowly wind their way back towards the carriage.

This, Timothy thought to himself, a smile lingering on his lips, had been a most interesting—and wonderful—afternoon.

CHAPTER TEN

Taking in a deep breath, Delilah lifted her chin and tried to smile as she stepped inside the ballroom, knowing that by now, news of her engagement was known to all contained within. Gossip had spread all across London in what had felt like a matter of minutes, and by the evening, her uncle had come to dinner to inform her that he had heard of her engagement and, whilst he was pleased to know of it, he was frustrated that she had not told him herself.

There had been a day now for the news to continue all around London and stepping in front of the *ton*, Delilah knew that everyone would be interested in her attendance this evening. They would look at her and know precisely who she was and who she was engaged to, and if they did not, then someone would inform them almost at once.

Her cheeks grew hot as she heard a whisper from someone near to her, but with an effort, Delilah kept herself facing straight ahead, refusing to look at the person speaking.

"Lord Coventry will be here with you very soon," Lady Newfield murmured, walking alongside Delilah as they progressed through the room. "And Lord Robertson is also expected to be here this evening."

Delilah nodded, seeing a small gap amongst the guests and making her way towards it, hoping that she might be able to hide herself away in the shadows for a short time. Lady Newfield went with her and within a few minutes, Delilah no longer felt as though she were the sole object of attention within the room. Letting out a long breath that she had not even known she had been holding, Delilah felt a weakness climb all through her and sat down heavily in an available chair.

"You did very well," Lady Newfield murmured as the conversations around her continued in earnest. "I am sure Lord Coventry will be with us soon."

"No doubt his presence will bring a good deal more attention to me," Delilah replied, a little despairingly. She had prepared herself as best she could for this evening, had tried to find the very same courage that had filled her when she had spoken to Lady Parrington. Whilst she had been able to walk across the floor without stumbling, without looking about, and without showing any visible signs of embarrassment, inwardly, she had been deeply anxious and afraid.

"It will," Lady Newfield agreed, speaking candidly. "But you must prepare yourself for this. I do not think that the rumors and gossip will even *begin* to abate until you are wed."

Delilah nodded but said nothing, feeling her heart quake just a little within her as she tried to tell herself that she would manage to do all that was required of her so long as she had Lord Coventry and Lady Newfield by her side.

"At least my uncle is happy," she muttered as Lady Newfield's brows knitted together. "He spoke to me last evening."

"He has not hurt you again, I hope?" Lady Newfield began, but Delilah quickly shook her head.

"I do not think he dares, given what Lord Coventry threatened," she said, a little wryly. "Not that Lord Coventry would not marry me, of course, but rather that my uncle would not gain all that he had been promised."

Lady Newfield sank into a chair, her eyes searching Delilah's face—to the point that Delilah felt as though her godmother was looking into her very soul.

"You feel something for Lord Coventry, I think, Delilah," Lady Newfield said with a quietness in her voice that told Delilah her godmother already knew what had passed between herself and Lord Coventry. "And he for you?"

Not quite certain what to say, Delilah could only nod, looking away from Lady Newfield, a little disconcerted.

"I am very glad for you," Lady Newfield said, a smile lighting her eyes. "Despite my reservations, it appears that Lord Coventry is an excellent gentleman and will, I think, care for you very deeply."

"I believe he will, yes," Delilah said, her anxiety blown away by the gladness in her heart as she thought of

Lord Coventry. "I was so very afraid when I first received my uncle's letter, but now I believe that I am very fortunate indeed."

"Do excuse me for interrupting you both."

Delilah looked up quickly and then hurriedly rose to her feet. "Good evening, Lord Robertson," she said as Lady Newfield rose also. "Might I present Lady Newfield? My godmother."

Quickly introductions were made, and soon it became apparent the reason for Lord Robertson's presence.

"I should very much like to dance with you, Miss Mullins," Lord Robertson said with a gleam in his eye. "Do you have any free to which I might put my name?"

Delilah flushed as she handed Lord Robertson her dance card. She did not want to dance with him, for she feared that the reason for him coming to seek her out was so that he might then be caught up with gossip, so that people might flock to him to speak to him of what he knew of the infamous Miss Mullins. Lady Newfield clearly knew of it also, for her eyes narrowed as she glared at Lord Robertson, who eagerly wrote his name down for first the quadrille, and thereafter, the waltz, which came a short time later.

"The quadrille will begin in just a moment!" he exclaimed, looking thoroughly delighted with himself. "Shall we, Miss Mullins?"

Delilah had no excuse, no reason to remain where she was. Her stomach swirling with nerves, she took Lord Robertson's proffered arm and allowed him to lead her onto the floor.

Fully aware that everyone present might well be looking at her, Delilah fought off her nerves with all the strength she could muster. Lord Robertson seemed to be reveling in it, grinning broadly and turning his head from left to right so that everyone would notice him. Delilah kept her head low and her eyes fixed to somewhere near Lord Robertson's feet. She did not look left and right to the others in the set for fear of what they would say to her, the looks she would receive. When the music began, it came as something of a relief, for she was finally able to concentrate on the steps rather than on the nerves that were running through her.

Lord Robertson laughed and smiled the entire way through, but Delilah could feel none of the same joy. With every second that passed, all she could do was pray that soon, the dance would be over and she would no longer have to remain in the middle of the ballroom where everyone could see her.

"Thank you for a wonderful dance, Miss Mullins."

She curtsied and tried to smile as Lord Robertson bowed and rose again with a flourish.

"I do hope you enjoyed it," Lord Robertson continued, making no effort to take her back to Lady Newfield but seeming to linger to keep them both where they were. The other couples moved around in front of them, a myriad of colors. "The waltz will begin soon."

"I should return to Lady Newfield," Delilah murmured, but still, Lord Robertson did not move. Eventually, as she arched one eyebrow and gestured towards where he was to take her, he finally laughed loudly again, although Delilah did not see what it was that he found so mirthful. "But of course," he said, and finally, offered her his arm.

"I was speaking to your Lord Coventry earlier this evening, you know," he said as he walked slowly back, their steps seeming to drag. "I was most delighted to converse with him."

Delilah's heart slammed into her chest, but she tried not to react visibly.

"We talked for some time," Lord Robertson continued, sounding almost gleeful. "And thereafter, I thought that I simply had to come and find you so that I might convey my congratulations on your engagement."

"That is very kind of you," Delilah murmured, wondering why Lord Coventry had not yet managed to come to speak to her given that he was present. "I appreciate your kindness, Lord Robertson."

Lord Robertson looked pleased at this remark but said nothing, allowing them to walk in silence the rest of the way. However, when they arrived back to where Delilah had been sitting, there was no sign of Lady Newfield.

"How very strange," Lord Robertson murmured, looking all around him as though Lady Newfield was hiding somewhere. "I did think that she—"

"Miss Mullins?"

Delilah turned her head to see Miss Jamieson approaching, her eyes a little concerned as she hurried forward, reaching to take both of Delilah's hands in her own.

"Good evening, Miss Jamieson," Delilah replied quickly. "Is something wrong?"

Miss Jamieson shook her head. "No, indeed not. I merely wanted to ascertain how *you* fared, given the situation that you find yourself in at present."

Delilah smiled at her friend but let go of her hands. "I see," she replied, appreciating Miss Jamieson's thoughtfulness. "I am quite all right, I assure you."

"If you ladies will excuse me." Lord Robertson bowed and turned away, a smile still playing about his lips and his duty, evidently, now completed since he had returned Delilah to someone, even if it was not Lady Newfield. Delilah watched him go without expression, her heart sinking heavily as she closed her eyes, knowing that Lord Robertson would soon be back to dance the waltz with her.

"He comes to seek your attention so that he might garner the attention of the *ton* for himself," Miss Jamieson said with a grim smile. "A foolish gentleman, that one."

"One that is easily manipulated, certainly," Delilah agreed. "However, he did mention that Lord Coventry is here, and as yet, I have not seen him." She worried her lip but Miss Jamieson merely shrugged.

"I am sure he will find you when he is able," she said. "No doubt he is caught up with much conversation and the like over his engagement to you." She smiled and Delilah tried to nod her agreement but felt her heart drop all the lower. "Perhaps he hopes for the whispers to die down a little before he comes to join you."

"That may be so," Delilah agreed, her voice a little dulled. "But now it seems I cannot find Lady Newfield either."

Miss Jamieson's expression became one of concern. "Lady Newfield is gone?"

"I—I left her here," Delilah replied, gesturing to the chairs to her left. "Lady Newfield was most insistent that Lord Robertson return me to her, so I cannot imagine why she would have simply departed, knowing that I would return at any moment."

"Then mayhap we should look for her," Miss Jamieson replied, offering Delilah her arm. "She must be within the ballroom someplace."

To step away, to wander back through the guests, and to know that they were all watching her again made Delilah's heart tremble, but she nodded and took Miss Jamieson's arm. Miss Jamieson smiled and began to walk slowly but with purpose, looking from left to right as she did so, whilst Delilah did all she could to push aside her fears and to hold her head high.

There was, thankfully, another dance now beginning, and so couples came to step onto the floor as Delilah and Miss Jamieson made their way forward. When the music began, they hurried to move from the dance floor, not wanting to be in the way—and as they did so, someone caught Delilah's eye.

"Lord Coventry!"

He was standing with his feet planted firmly apart, his head held high and his arms crossed across his chest. His jaw was set, and his eyes dark, and it only took Delilah a moment to realize why.

Lady Parrington.

"Look," she murmured, slowing Miss Jamieson's steps. "Lord Coventry."

Miss Jamieson stopped and looked to where Delilah now gestured. "Indeed," she commented, sounding a little surprised. "And Lady Parrington."

"I do not think it is a happy conversation," Delilah remarked as Miss Jamieson nodded. "Should I go to him?"

Miss Jamieson shook her head. "I do not think it would do you much good, Miss Mullins. Will she not then begin to pierce you with her words also?"

Delilah hesitated, then sighed and nodded her head. "Yes, I believe she would."

"Then there is no need for you to do so," Miss Jamieson answered with a small shrug. "But as for myself..." She lifted one eyebrow and smiled at Delilah. "If you will wait, I will go and speak to him and try to draw him away from Lady Parrington."

Awash with relief, Delilah let go of her friend's arm. "I would be very glad indeed if you would do so," she agreed, taking a few steps back so that she now stood near to the wall rather than near to Lord Coventry. "I will remain here."

Miss Jamieson smiled and then turned on her heel to walk back towards Lady Parrington and Lord Coventry. Delilah twisted her fingers together as she watched, praying that her friend would succeed so that Lord Coventry could come to join them. She needed his help to find Lady Newfield. The fact that she still could not find the lady made her afraid, for she could not understand why she had simply disappeared.

"Good evening, Miss Mullins." A gentleman bowed

before her. "Lord Chesterton. Just in case you do not recall my name."

She frowned. "Good evening." Her brow furrowed as she tried to recall whether or not she had ever been introduced to this particular gentleman before. She did not think that she had, but he spoke with such an ease of manner that it came across as though they had spoken previously and perhaps at great length. However, given how much Lord Coventry had spoken of Lord Chesterton, Delilah knew precisely who she was now speaking to. "If you are looking for your sister, then I am glad to inform you that she is speaking with Lord Coventry." She gestured towards them but Lord Chesterton did not so much as glance at them.

"Lady Newfield took ill whilst you were showing off on the dance floor with Lord Robertson," he said, a small, dark smile pulling at one side of his mouth. "I thought it best to come and inform you at once."

Delilah's frown remained, and whilst she was a little worried now about what had happened to Lady Newfield, a large part of her remained entirely wary. What was Lord Chesterton now trying to do? Attempting to have her go in search of Lady Newfield, only to be pulled into a trap? The same had been done to Lord Coventry, and therefore, Delilah did not immediately believe Lord Chesterton.

"That is unfortunate," she said, letting out a sigh. "Where did she go to rest?"

Lord Chesterton shrugged. "I believe she wanted to return home and is now waiting for you in her carriage," he said as Delilah continued to nod as though she believed every word. "You should go to her just as soon as you can."

"I shall go once I am ready," Delilah replied easily. "But I thank you for coming to speak to me of her where-abouts, Lord Chesterton. That is very good of you."

For a moment, Lord Chesterton stared back at Delilah, his brow furrowing and his jaw working furi-ously as though he wanted to say something more to her, wanted to get her to hurry after Lady Newfield at once. But Delilah remained precisely where she was, her heart pounding and her stomach tight as she looked back into Lord Chesterton's face, refusing to do what he expected her to do.

"But of course," Lord Chesterton muttered eventu-ally, lowering his head in a small bow before turning away from her. Delilah watched him leave, her heart beating much too quickly and her mind clouded with fear as to what had occurred to Lady Newfield. But still, she waited, feeling her instincts tell her to remain precisely where she was, to fight against the urge to follow after Lord Chesterton and go directly to the carriage where Lady Newfield was supposedly waiting.

Her lip caught between her teeth as she saw Lady Parrington throw her head back and laugh, although the sound was not a welcome one. Miss Jamieson stood stiffly, but after a moment, Delilah saw her bob a curtsy and turn away from the lady—and with her came Lord Coventry. Lady Parrington turned her head to watch them leave, finally catching Delilah's eyes. She smirked, but Delilah lifted her chin and glared back at the lady, refusing to be cowed in any way. It took some moments but, eventually, Lady Parrington turned her head away again and then made her way towards the crowd of guests.

"Miss Mullins." Lord Coventry was at her side in moments, his hands reaching out for hers. "I have tried to come to your side more than once this evening but have been prevented by first Lord Robertson—who simply would not stop speaking to me—and then by Lady Parrington, as you have now seen." He squeezed her fingers but let them go. "You did not come to speak to the lady, Miss Mullins. That was wise." Wincing as though the words that had been flung at him by Lady Parrington had left jagged wounds all over him, he continued, "She is still displeased that we are to wed."

"Because she wanted you to have a life of solitude?" Miss Jamieson asked, looking a little confused as she glanced from Lord Coventry to Delilah and back again. "She was not satisfied with you merely being viewed as unworthy by the majority of the *ton*?"

"It would seem that she was not," Delilah answered with a shake of her head. "She is quite determined to bring you down to the depths, Lord Coventry, in any way she can."

Lord Coventry shook his head and closed his eyes for a moment. "It is as though I never knew her," he said as though speaking entirely to himself. "It is very strange to now think of the lady in question as the one I once cared for so very much."

Something about what he said made Delilah's heart drop to the floor and then hit her back hard in the chest. She did not know what to say for a moment, wanting to tell Lord Coventry that she was very glad to hear him speak in such a way and yet, at the same time, finding it very difficult to form the words that were required.

"And now we have the worry regarding Lady Newfield," Miss Jamieson added when no one spoke. Turning to Delilah, she frowned. "I saw Lord Chesterton speak to you also. Did he say something about her?"

Lord Coventry frowned, looking back at Delilah with a worried gaze. "Do you mean to say that there is something wrong with Lady Newfield?" he asked, frowning. "Where is she?"

"I—I do not know," Delilah answered truthfully. "I have been looking for her ever since my dance with Lord Robertson. When I returned to where she was meant to be, I found that she was gone." Her heart began to quicken with a sense of panic, but she fought it. "Lord Chesterton came to speak to me, however."

"Lord Chesterton?" Lord Coventry said sharply, his brow furrowing all the more. "Why was he—?"

Delilah put a hand on his arm. "He came to inform me that Lady Newfield has taken ill," she said by way of explanation. "And that she is has gone to her carriage to return home. I am apparently requested to join her."

"Then you must go!" Miss Jamieson exclaimed, but Delilah shook her head.

"No, Miss Jamieson, I must be on my guard," she said, trying to explain without stating too much about what she suspected. "Recall that Lord Chesterton has already attempted to harm Lord Coventry by claiming that he injured him without cause." She lifted one shoulder. "And his sister, Lady Parrington, does not want Lord

Coventry to have any joy." Briefly, she told Miss Jamieson about the very strong reaction that had come from Lady Parrington when she had first heard of Lord Coventry's engagement. Miss Jamieson's eyes widened and her cheeks paled just a little.

"So," Miss Jamieson said slowly, "you believe, therefore, that something untoward might occur if you go in search of Lady Newfield alone?"

Delilah nodded. "That is it precisely, Miss Jamieson," she said as Lord Coventry reached out to touch Delilah's fingers with his own, his expression grave. "I did not want to go with Lord Chesterton to find Lady Newfield, only to discover that it was not as he said."

"You are being cautious," Lord Coventry muttered, rubbing one hand over his eyes. "That is wise, Miss Mullins. Although, I should inform you that I spoke at length to Lord Robertson earlier this evening." His hand dropped to his side, and he looked at her steadily. "He informed me of the name of the lady he had been intending to see the night of the great assembly." Delilah saw his eyes slide towards Miss Jamieson before returning to her, clearly a little uncertain as to whether or not he should say more in front of the lady.

"Please," Delilah said, a little breathlessly. "Who was it?"

Miss Jamieson looked confused, putting a hand on Delilah's arm. "Is there something wrong?" she asked as Delilah continued to look up into Lord Coventry's face. "I do not feel as though I understand all that is going on."

Lord Coventry held Delilah's gaze and did not answer Miss Jamieson. "It was Lady Fenella."

Delilah caught her breath, her hand flying to her mouth as her eyes widened. "Can it be?" she whispered, not understanding in the least. "Surely, she cannot be..."

"What is it that you are speaking of, Miss Mullins?" Miss Jamieson asked, sounding quite exasperated. "I do not understand!"

Delilah turned to her friend, shaking her head. "There is too much to explain at present," she said, still wanting to keep as much of what had been happening to herself. "We must find Lady Newfield. I believe, however, that you and I, Lord Coventry, should be very careful around Lord and Lady Parrington, as well as Lord Chesterton."

Lord Coventry held her gaze for a long moment, his expression troubled, and then, finally, he nodded. "I understand."

"We cannot be certain of anything as yet," Delilah reminded him, reaching out to take his hand in hers so that she might comfort him in some way. "But I do think that it would be wise to be very cautious indeed."

He nodded, his brow still furrowed, and worry written into the grooved lines of his forehead. "Then we should go to the carriage, yes?"

"It is the only place I can think to look," Delilah answered, feeling herself growing a little desperate. "But I fear she will not be there, for the expectation is that I shall be present alone, seeking her and eager to depart so that she might recover at home. When I reach the carriage, I do not expect her actually to be present at all."

"Then we shall attend together," Miss Jamieson answered, her voice determined even though Delilah knew she would still be confused by all that was going on. "The three of us together will ensure that you are quite safe, Miss Mullins."

Closing her eyes for a moment, Delilah nodded and tried to smile. "I shall be contented with any plan, just so long as we find my godmother."

"We will," Lord Coventry answered as Delilah took Miss Jamieson's arm and began to slowly make her way across the ballroom.

CHAPTER ELEVEN

Timothy set his jaw as he followed after Miss Mullins and Miss Jamieson. He had not enjoyed this evening thus far, having been the center of attention from the moment he had stepped inside. He had little doubt that Miss Mullins had found it difficult also, for she would have been noticed by almost everyone.

His jaw worked hard as he battled the sudden anger that had burned in his veins when the lovely Lady Parrington—or the once lovely Lady Margaret—had come to speak to him. The vile words that had come from her lips had not only shocked him but made him question, for what was the second time, what he had ever seen in her. He had once wanted to marry her. There was none of that in him now. Rather, all that was left was a deep sense of regret that he had ever allowed her into his heart.

Stepping out into the hallway, he saw Miss Mullins and Miss Jamieson hurry forward, although he had to avoid one or two others seemingly returning to the ball-room. Thinking to catch up with the ladies as soon as he could, Timothy hesitated for a moment, getting the attention of a nearby footman.

"You there," he said as the footman snapped to attention. "Have you been standing here for most of the evening?"

The footman nodded, his face impassive. "Yes, my lord."

"And did you see an older lady leaving recently?" Timothy asked as the two ladies disappeared out of the house. "She was making for her carriage, I believe."

The footman shook his head, looking a little confused. "I did not," he answered slowly, frowning. "There has not been an older lady alone leaving the house."

Timothy made to follow after the ladies, only for something the footman had said suddenly slamming into his mind. "Wait a moment," he said slowly, coming back to look at the footman. "Do you mean to say that a lady such as I have described left the house with someone else?"

Nodding, the footman cleared his throat, his hands behind his back. "She was accompanied by a lady and a gentleman, my lord," he said, looking confused. "I presumed they were—"

"Thank you," Timothy said sharply before moving quickly towards the front door to catch up with both Miss Mullins and Miss Jamieson. To his relief, they had not gone far, for they were both standing on the steps that led down from the house to the road, staring straight ahead at a carriage that was waiting for them. The door was open and, as Timothy hurried forward, he saw that there were no occupants inside.

"What has happened?" he breathed, only for Miss Mullins to put a hand on his arm.

"A gentleman was within," she whispered, looking up at him, her eyes filling with tears. "But that is Lady Newfield's carriage, certainly."

Timothy's breath caught. "A gentleman?"

"The moment he saw that there were two of us present here, he flung himself from the carriage and ran out to the street," Miss Jamieson said, her face looking all the more pale in the moonlight. "I am sure that, had Miss Mullins been alone, he would have caught her tightly and refused to let her go."

"Thus ruining my reputation and bringing an end to our engagement," Miss Mullins finished, her voice tremulous. "You would have refused to have wed me."

He shook his head. "I would have understood."

"Perhaps those who set about this plan did not think you would have such an intention," Miss Jamieson suggested, looking sympathetically at Miss Mullins. "No doubt someone would have been prepared to come and see the situation, bringing news of Miss Mullins' shame to everyone."

Closing his eyes, Timothy battled the anger that began to bubble up within him, feeling furious at what had been attempted against his betrothed. "I did have to pass a few other guests returning to the ballroom," he said, his words forced out from between gritted teeth. "Any one of them could have been involved and would have departed almost the moment they saw you *both* approaching."

"I am very grateful to you, Miss Jamieson," Miss Mullins murmured, as Miss Jamieson reached out and squeezed her hand. "That could have been a very bad situation, indeed."

His anger now a little more controlled, Timothy took in a long breath. "I spoke to a footman. He stated that he saw an older lady departing the house with another lady and a gentleman." Looking all about him, he saw no sign of either Lady Newfield or the other two.

Miss Jamieson huffed out a breath, her hands planted on her hips. "There is something gravely wrong, is there not, Lord Coventry?" She looked from one of them to the next, a small frown on her forehead. "I must know all. Please."

"I think," Timothy began, slowly, seeing how Miss Mullins trembled slightly, "that perhaps Miss Mullins suspects that Lord Chesterton—perhaps with the help of his sister—are still, for whatever reason, attempting to have me thrown from society."

Miss Mullins nodded and, before he could even offer her his support, she leaned into him. "I am sure that it is the case," she said, looking up at him as he slid his arm about her waist. "Lady Fenella is acquainted with Lady Parrington. Indeed, we saw her out walking with her one afternoon, Miss Jamieson, did we not?"

Miss Jamieson nodded, her brow still lowered. "Indeed, although she appeared to be very docile. Lady Parrington clearly wanted to have as much of our attention as she could."

"Which she got without hesitation, for Lady Fenella moved a little further away from us, did she not?" Miss Mullins asked as Miss Jamieson nodded. "Little doubt then that Lady Parrington could do with the lady as she wished. Mayhap her brother, Lord Chesterton, was eager to set up a particular trap for you, Lord Coventry." Her eyes were troubled as she spoke aloud, trying to understand what had occurred. "Lady Parrington easily manipulated Lady Fenella. In turn, she then encouraged Lady Fenella to pay attention to Lord Robertson, knowing him to be the sort of gentleman who needs very little encouragement in such matters."

"Then used her as bait for Lord Robertson on the night of the great assembly," Timothy murmured as Miss Mullins looked up at him, nodding. "With Lord Chesterton ready to strike him the moment he came in. I would suspect that Lord Chesterton was the one who asked the footman to send word to me to attend Lord Holland in the blue room."

Drawing in a long, shaky breath, Miss Mullins closed her eyes and nodded. "Lord Chesterton used his sister, and in turn, she used Lady Fenella. All to bring you lower, Lord Coventry, so that you could never again be a part of London society." Her words seemed to hang in the air, making them all the more ominous.

"What I do not understand," Miss Jamieson began, looking thoroughly confused, "is why Lord Chesterton would do such a thing. Did you ever discover the truth behind his claim that you had beaten him in such a manner?"

Timothy had to shake his head. "I have not."

"And I am all the more surprised that Lady Parrington would be involved," Miss Jamieson continued. "I was quite certain that you and she cared deeply for each other, Lord Coventry."

Again, Timothy had nothing to do but nod. He could not understand why, if their theory were correct, the lady he had once been so close to would choose to help her brother and do such a thing to him.

"It may be that she has no other choice," he said with a shrug. "Mayhap, there is more to Lord Chesterton than we realize."

There came a moment or two of silence as the ladies considered this.

"I suppose that there may well be an opportunity soon to ask her about such a thing," Miss Mullins said as she leaned against him all the more. "But first, we must find Lord Chesterton, must we not?"

Timothy nodded, praying that he would be able to keep his temper when it came to securing Lord Chesterton's attention. The last thing he needed to do was to allow his anger loose when there were a great many answers required. "Come, Miss Mullins," he said as gently as he could. "You need to rest."

She shook her head as she moved a little away from him. "What I need, Lord Coventry, is to find my godmother."

Glad, in some ways, to see her determination and courage evidencing itself more and more and yet sorrowful that she had cause for such a thing, Timothy nodded and offered her his arm. With a small, sad smile, Miss Mullins took it at once, and together, the three of them began to walk back inside to where the ball continued.

~

"DELILAH!"

It was with complete and utter shock that Timothy saw Lady Newfield standing just inside the ballroom door, her face as white as milk. She reached out and grasped Miss Mullins' hands, pulling her from Timothy's side and then embracing her so tightly that Miss Mullins coughed hard as she was released.

"Lady—Lady Newfield?" Timothy queried, staring at the older lady as she, in turn, stared at Miss Mullins. "Where have you been? We have been desperate with worry."

Lady Newfield reached out and touched Miss Mullins' cheek. "I thought you were unwell! That you had collapsed and—"

"I am quite well, Lady Newfield," Miss Mullins replied, looking thoroughly confused. "I was told that *you* had been taken ill and required me to return to the carriage so that we might return home at once."

Timothy grimaced as Lady Newfield sucked in a breath, her eyes flaring with sudden horror.

"I was quite safe, however," Miss Mullins said quickly as Lady Newfield closed her eyes tightly, swaying just a little. "Miss Jamieson and Lord Coventry were with me, and together, we went to the carriage."

"Might I ask," Timothy interrupted, leading Miss Mullins, Miss Jamieson, and Lady Newfield a little away from the door of the ballroom so that they would not be overheard. "Might I ask who spoke to you, Lady Newfield? Who told you that she had been taken ill?"

Lady Newfield's eyes turned to his and she looked at him for some moments before she spoke. "I...I confess I do not know," she whispered, one hand now pressed to her heart. "I was only told that Delilah had collapsed at the end of the quadrille and had been taken out of the room. The lady offered to take me to her, and of course, I went without hesitation."

"Where did you go?" Miss Mullins asked quietly. "To another room in the townhouse?"

Lady Newfield shook her head. "It took us some minutes to remove ourselves from the ballroom. The lady I was with took a great deal of time making any progress whatsoever, and we did seem to take an inordinately long time to move through the crowd." Closing her eyes, she bit her lip for a moment before continuing. "When we reached the hallway, a gentleman appeared. Obviously, he had been waiting for the lady, for he hurried over to her at once. Once the lady told this gentleman who I was —and I am angry now that I was not wise enough to ask for their names—he informed me that Miss Mullins had recovered significantly and that she had fainted due to the intense heat in the ballroom. She had begged to go for a short walk in the cold air and had been accompanied by a lady and a gentleman." She gestured to Timothy. "I presumed you and perhaps Miss Jamieson had gone with her. And so, the lady and gentleman I was with walked out with me, but we could not find you anywhere."

Timothy frowned. "And you returned to the ball through the front door?"

Lady Newfield shook her head, her face filling with color. "I foolishly believed the lady when she suggested you might have gone through the servants' entrance not to make a scene upon your return. Truly, my dear girl, I am not usually as thoughtless as this, but I was very frantic indeed to find you again."

Miss Mullins smiled gently and took Lady Newfield's hands again. "I am quite all right, as you can see."

"And so you returned to the ballroom another way," Timothy said, wanting to make certain he understood everything. "Might I ask where this lady and gentlemen went thereafter?"

Lady Newfield waved a hand impatiently. "They told me they would speak to Lord Robertson, who had been with you when you had collapsed, although they were not sure where he was at present," she said. "I was so very upset that I said I would wait by the door to make certain he would not depart without my being aware of him."

"And now here we are," Miss Mullins finished with a wry smile. "It appears that the intention to throw guilt all over my shoulders has been thoroughly shattered."

"Thanks to your wisdom," Timothy told her, seeing how Lady Newfield squeezed her goddaughter's hand. "You knew not to follow Lord Chesterton when he told you of Lady Newfield's supposed illness. I do not think that he expected you to be so wise, Miss Mullins."

Lady Newfield drew in a shuddering breath, her

shoulders settling. "I am so very grateful to you all," she said, looking at Miss Jamieson and then to Timothy himself. "I behaved in a foolish manner whilst you all appear to have behaved with great purpose and consideration." She looked at her goddaughter, tears swimming in her eyes. "I am very relieved, indeed."

Timothy took in a long breath, looking all about the ballroom and finding himself deeply frustrated. He could attempt to seek out Lord Chesterton this evening, to throw the weight of his accusations upon the man's shoulders—but there would not be any real opportunity to discuss the matter in its entirety. He would need Lady Parrington to be present also, and even, mayhap, Lady Fenella. This evening did not seem to be the best time for him to do so, despite his urgency.

"I think," he said as Miss Mullins turned to him, "that it might be best to consider all that has happened and find a way to speak to Lord Chesterton and Lady Parrington without distraction."

Miss Mullins' expression fell.

"I should like to do so this evening, but I do not think it wise," he said honestly. "I have an idea as to how to make the arrangements so that they are all present. Have no fear, Miss Mullins. Within a few days, we shall be able to find out precisely what has been going on and why Lord Chesterton has been so eager to punish me in this way." Looking at Miss Jamieson, he smiled. "Might we be able to arrange the visit at your father's townhouse?" he asked, seeing how her brows rose, her eyes widening just a fraction. "I believe, Miss Jamieson, that they will attend you without hesitation. Whereas, if any of us were to do so, the invitation would be thoroughly ignored."

Miss Jamieson nodded, her hands held tightly in front of her, her fingers threaded together. "I shall make the arrangements this evening, once I return," she said firmly. "Shall we say in two days' time?"

He nodded as Miss Mullins and Lady Newfield did the same. "Two days," he repeated, his breath easing out of his chest as a new resolve filled him. "And then, finally, all shall be made known."

CHAPTER TWELVE

"Miss Mullins."

Reaching out to take her hand, Timothy felt his heart quicken, aware of just how much he owed her, how much he had come to care for her. Her nearness brought fresh joy to his heart despite the difficult circumstances.

"Good afternoon, Lord Coventry," she said as Lady Newfield eased the door closed behind them, having been shown in only moments before by an anxious-looking Miss Jamieson. "You are prepared for this meeting, I hope?"

Seeing how Lady Newfield had wandered to the window and was now steadfastly looking out at the street below, Timothy gave in to his urgings and pulled Miss Mullins closer, his arms about her waist. She fell lightly against his chest, clearly a little surprised at his boldness, and looked up at him with her lips slightly parted.

Heat shot through his core as he fought the urge to press his lips to hers. There was more to be done before he could even consider such a thing, before he could have the joyous moments with her when he could tell her all that was in his heart.

"I have missed you these last two days," he said softly, seeing how her eyes shone and her lips curved gently. "It has been almost torturous sitting alone in my townhouse, wondering about where you are and what you are doing."

Her smile grew. "If it is of any comfort, Lord Coventry," she said, one hand pressed against his chest, "I have done very little other than think of you."

Hope burned in his heart as he pulled one hand from her waist and touched her cheek. When he had signed the agreement with her uncle, he had done so with an awareness that he was doing so simply to gain what he required to continue his family line. He had never once expected to gain such a lady as Miss Mullins, whose fear and reticence had melted away into newfound courage and determination. The kindness in her eyes, the gentleness in her manner, and the sweetness of her character made him feel as though he were gaining much more than just a wife. He was gaining a true friend, a companion through life, and, indeed, a lady he could love without hesitation.

"When this matter is at an end, Miss Mullins," he began—only for her to shake her head, her eyes closing tightly for a moment. Confused, he cleared his throat and made to step back, but Miss Mullins only smiled.

"Can you not call me 'Delilah,' Coventry?" she asked, speaking in more of an easy manner with him than she had ever done before. "We are to be wed very soon, are we not?"

The smile that spread across his face was one of sheer delight. "I should like nothing more, *Delilah*," he said, seeing how she blushed as he spoke her name. "What I was to say is that, when this matter is at an end, Delilah, I should like to speak to you of our future." Pressing one hand to his heart, he held her gaze and wondered if she could see in his eyes the longing that was growing steadily within him. "I have much that I wish to share with you."

Reaching up, Miss Mullins tentatively pressed her hand over his. "I should be glad to listen to you whenever you wish to speak to me of it, Coventry," she told him, her eyes shining. "For I believe that I have just as much to share with you."

Had Lady Newfield not been present, Timothy would have lowered his head and kissed her, and, as such, the battle that fought within him was difficult indeed. But, eventually, he nodded, stepped back, and let his hands fall to his sides.

"Then let us hope that we are able to bring matters to a close very soon," he said as she smiled her agreement, her eyes twinkling.

"Hush!" Lady Newfield came hurrying across the floor, her feet barely making a sound as she drew near to them. "I can hear voices."

In an instant, everything changed. Timothy froze in place as Miss Mullins turned slowly towards the door. Lady Newfield was quite correct. There came the voice of Lady Parrington and, chiming in on occasion, came another, lower voice that Timothy recognized as Lord Chesterton. They walked past the room that they waited in and, as they listened, Timothy heard the butler announce them to Miss Jamieson.

The time was at hand.

"We wait for a few minutes until they have settled themselves," Lady Newfield murmured, reminding them of what they all already knew. "Then, we shall enter."

"I will wait by the door," Timothy muttered. "Miss Mullins make sure to stay by Lady Newfield's side. That will be the safest place for you."

She nodded, her color a little pale but that shine of determination beginning to grow in her eyes. Timothy closed his eyes and waited, taking in long breaths and letting them out with great care, knowing that he had to be very cautious in what came next.

Lady Newfield touched his arm, and Timothy opened his eyes. She nodded once, and he stepped forward immediately, with Miss Mullins catching his gaze for just a moment.

He could not help himself. Turning around, he caught Miss Mullins' hand and brought it to his lips.

"It will be at an end soon," he told her, seeing how her eyes fastened to his. "Are you quite prepared?"

Miss Mullins swallowed hard but nodded. "I am."

Lifting her hand to his mouth, he kissed the back of her hand and then turned to face the door. Setting his shoulders, he opened it carefully and, making as little noise as possible, the three of them stepped out into the corridor. It was just as well that Miss Jamieson's father did not intend to join them, else he might wonder why Lady Newfield, the suitable chaperone for this afternoon tea, had come out of an entirely different room from his daughter!

Moving carefully forward, Timothy looked over his shoulder and saw Lady Newfield and Miss Mullins just behind him. He reached for the door handle and, after a moment, turned it and threw the door open wide. Striding forward, he stepped aside so that Miss Mullins and Lady Newfield could move ahead of him before catching the door and closing it again tightly, leaning back against it. Only then did he survey the scene before him.

The dining room table had been laid out with a great many delicacies, and Miss Jamieson was in the middle of pouring tea. She did not even glance up at them but continued do to so without even pausing, although Timothy noticed that her hand shook just a little as she held the teapot. His brows rose as he realized it was not only Lady Parrington sitting at the table, but also her husband as well as her brother. It seemed that they were to have a very cozy conversation this afternoon.

"I do hope you do not mind," Miss Jamieson said as she set the teapot down carefully, "but I have invited some other guests for this particular afternoon. I am sure we will have a good deal to discuss together."

Lady Parrington rose at once, her chair making a harsh grating sound on the floor such was the abruptness of her movement.

"I do not wish to be in the same *room* as this gentle-man!" she exclaimed, making to move towards the door. "Parrington!"

"Sit down, Lady Parrington," Lady Newfield said,

her voice echoing through the room and holding such a firmness that even Timothy himself felt a little cowed. Lady Parrington turned to look at Lady Newfield, that arrogant, haughty look still lingering on her face, but Lady Newfield did not even flinch.

"Sit down at once!" Lady Newfield said again, her voice even louder than before. "There is much we need to discuss, Lady Parrington, and I am quite certain that *you* will be able to provide us with many of the answers."

"As will you, Lord Chesterton," Timothy said, taking a few steps forward as Lady Parrington sat back down in her chair—albeit with a look of fury on her face. "I believe we should begin with the explanation I have been longing for."

Lord Chesterton lifted his chin, his lip curled but, as Timothy held his gaze, he saw the way that the gentleman's eyes flickered.

"I want to know why you told the *ton* that I was the one to attack you that evening," he said, leaning on the back of a chair and looking at the gentleman he had once called a friend. "I am fully aware that I was angry and upset at your refusal to allow me to marry your sister, but I never *once—*"

"You may have convinced your betrothed and her acquaintance that you did not do such a thing," Lord Chesterton interrupted, turning his head away from Timothy with a somewhat insolent air. "But I shall not agree with your pretense."

Timothy gritted his teeth and looked away. He had not expected Lord Chesterton to admit to anything, of course, but to have him be so immediately dismissive was galling.

"Then might I ask why you lied to me at the ball, Lord Chesterton?" he heard Miss Mullins say, seeing how she sat gracefully in a chair, her voice soft. "You told me that Lady Newfield had been taken ill and was waiting for me in the carriage so that we might return home. However, when I went to see, there was a gentleman sitting inside."

Lord Chesterton said nothing, although Timothy could see the way his jaw clenched hard.

"Thankfully, I had Miss Jamieson with me," Miss Mullins continued quietly. "Upon seeing us both approach, the fellow jumped out of the carriage and ran from us. Lady Newfield was nowhere to be seen, and I later discovered that she was quite safe and not at all unwell." She tilted her head as Timothy watched everyone at the table with sharp, careful eyes. "In fact, she had been told that I was the one who had been unwell."

"Thus, you spoke a complete and utter lie, Lord Chesterton," Lady Newfield said darkly. "What is your explanation for it?"

Lord Chesterton said nothing, his eyes darting from one person to the next, sweat beginning to bead on his brow.

"I was only telling you what I had heard," he replied eventually. "There can be nothing wrong with such a thing, surely? I was doing what I could to help."

Timothy shrugged. "Of course not," he said, seeing how Lord Chesterton shifted uncomfortably in his chair.

"So then, might I ask who you heard such a thing from? And why did they not come to speak to Miss Mullins?"

Silence fell over the group. No one spoke, and not a single sound was heard. Timothy felt the tension continue to mount, his hands tightening on the chair as he waited for Lord Chesterton to speak.

"You do not have an answer it seems," Lady Newfield said after a short time. "Which means that there is a reason that you have not yet shared, Lord Chesterton, as to why you have treated Lord Coventry so."

Much to Timothy's surprise, Lord Chesterton lifted his gaze and looked directly across the table towards his sister. Lady Parrington went a stark shade of red, which then immediately faded to gray.

"You involved your sister," Timothy remarked as Lord Chesterton's head snapped around towards him. "And for whatever reason, she agreed." One shoulder lifted and he shook his head. "It may trouble me a little, I confess, given that we once had what I thought was a shared affection between us, although I have, of course, found a greater love than I ever thought possible with Miss Mullins." He smiled at the lady, who looked at him and blushed, although her eyes were warm. "So, what did you have to say to make your sister behave so?" Tilting his head just a little, he looked directly at Lady Parrington. "Although you have become rather cruel since last Season, Lady Parrington. Perhaps you were more than willing to—"

"It was all her doing!"

The words flew from Lord Parrington's lips, and the entire room crashed into silence. Timothy stared at the gentleman, seeing how he had partially raised himself from his chair and now held out his hand, his finger pointed across the table towards his wife.

No one spoke. No one moved, and, as Timothy swiveled his gaze towards Lady Parrington, he was astonished to see just how pale she had gone. No longer had she the arrogant, smug smile on her face. Instead, her mouth was slack, her eyes wide with evident fear and her shoulders dropped low.

"It is true," Lord Chesterton said brokenly, his demeanor changed in an instant. His head hung low, his voice dark with pain as he spoke. "The night you spoke to me of your desire to marry my sister, I knew that I could not let you do so. We had been friends, and I was quite certain that you did not know the truth of her character."

Swallowing hard, Timothy felt a weakness grasp at him but forced himself to remain precisely where he was. This was almost too astonishing to believe.

"My sister attacked me," Lord Chesterton continued, his voice low and monotone. "Such was my shame that I did not know what else to do."

"Be silent, Chesterton!" Lady Parrington began to rise from her chair, but, as she did so, Lord Parrington stood up, thrusting his arm out towards Lady Parrington.

"Enough, Margaret!" he exclaimed, his face mottled with anger. "You have done—and said—enough!"

The atmosphere began to spark with tension, and for a moment, Timothy believed that Lady Parrington would strike out hard at Lord Parrington across the table. But, eventually, she sank back into her chair, her hands gripping the arms tightly.

"I have had enough," Lord Parrington muttered, speaking more than Timothy had ever heard before. "For a year, I have been forced to live in fear of my wife. Well, no longer!" He turned to Lord Chesterton. "No longer, Chesterton!"

Lord Chesterton covered his face with his hands.

"You are in fear of your wife?" Lady Newfield asked, sounding quite astonished. "For what reason?"

A groan came from Lord Chesterton, but after a moment, he dropped his hands and shook his head.

"The night I was attacked by my sister," Lord Chesterton said, "the night I told her that I had firmly decided that the marriage would not occur, Margaret demanded that I permit her to marry Lord Coventry." His eyes met Timothy's. "She did not care for you. She knew of your wealth. It was—and is—significant." Shaking his head, he dropped his gaze to the table again. "But still, I refused. There was nothing she could do."

"And yet you chose to blame Lord Coventry for your attack?"

"No," Lord Chesterton answered quickly, lifting his head. "No, indeed not." Rubbing one hand over his face, he closed his eyes tightly. "The following day, my sister wrote to Lord Coventry but received no reply."

Timothy twisted his lips. "I removed myself from the lady as quickly as I could. I returned the letter. I could not bear it, I told myself."

"That angered Margaret greatly," Lord Chesterton said, throwing a hand towards his sister, who had still not said a word, her lips pressed tightly together, her face white and drawn. "She went out that evening, although I remained at home. When she returned, it was as though the sister I had known was no longer." Lord Chesterton's voice grew hoarse as though he was reliving a terrible ordeal. "She asked me to join her for a short conversation before retiring to bed. What she said was something I shall never forget."

Lady Parrington shifted in her chair. "Be careful, brother," she hissed, but Lord Chesterton ignored her entirely.

"She told me that she had discovered the...acquaintance I had with Lady Foderingham," Lord Chesterton continued, his voice so quiet now that Timothy had to strain to hear him. "Lord Foderingham is one of my dearest friends. If the *beau monde* came to know of this, then I knew what would occur."

In an instant, everything became clear. Letting out a long breath, Timothy turned his eyes to Lady Parrington, the lady he had once thought himself in love with. "You stated that unless your brother did as you asked, you would reveal the truth to everyone."

Lady Parrington's lip curled. "You turned your back on me," she spat, one hand clenched as she crashed it down onto the table. "You rejected me. You did not fight for what might have been!"

"And so you sought to punish me by forcing your brother to blame your vicious attack on me," Timothy said, realizing now that he had not known Lady Parrington at all. "Upon returning to society, you despised me all the more, for not everyone in London believed what your brother had said."

Lord Parrington spoke up, his eyes like ice as they

fastened onto Lady Parrington. "She used us as pawns," he said, his voice rasping. "The debts I had were used against me. Lady Fenella was too shy and retiring to do anything but obey. Even Lord Robertson..." He shook his head, looking up at Timothy. "And when you escaped from her attempts, Lord Coventry, when she heard that you were engaged and to be happily wed, she then turned her attention on your betrothed."

"I did not want to do as she demanded," Lord Chesterton said, his voice humble as though he were begging Timothy for forgiveness. "But I had no choice."

Closing his eyes tightly, Timothy let air fill his lungs as he tried to clear his thoughts. But they did not, scrambling all around his mind as he fought to gain control.

"You did have a choice, Lord Chesterton," he heard Miss Mullins say, keeping his eyes closed and allowing the quietness of her voice to calm him. "But you chose to turn your back upon your friend and force what was your shame upon him instead."

Lord Chesterton made a choking noise, and Timothy opened his eyes, feeling his heart twist in his chest. Everything had become clear, and yet none of it brought any satisfaction. Instead, he felt only pain and regret, looking first at Lady Parrington and then at Lord Chesterton. It was all a dark, distorted mess.

"I will not say what you are to do next, Chesterton," he found himself saying, walking closer so that he was standing next to Miss Mullins. "For I find myself quite contented. I am betrothed to the most wonderful of ladies and intend to spend my days making certain that she has nothing but joy and love surrounding her. We will not often be in London, and I give no consideration to what the *beau monde* now thinks of me." Reaching down, he set one hand on Miss Mullins' shoulder and felt her fingers touch his hand, settling his heart all over again. "I will not say that I despise you, for I am grateful for your attempts to protect me from what would have been a disastrous marriage."

Turning his eyes to Lady Parrington, he set his jaw, seeing how her eyes flashed. "I did not ever really know you, Margaret. And I am glad now that I shall never have the opportunity. Our affection was nothing compared to what I now have in my heart—and to what I know is truly returned to me."

"You did not deserve me," Lady Parrington snapped, turning her head away, but Timothy did not give her even a momentary glance. There was nothing between them now, nothing that she could say that would affect his heart even a little.

"Shall we go, Miss Mullins?" he asked as she smiled up at him, her eyes clear. "I think I have had quite enough of all this."

"I am more than ready," she replied and, taking his hand, allowed him to lead her from the room. Lady Newfield excused herself quietly, thanked Miss Jamieson, and came after them, closing the door softly as they left the other occupants of the room behind them.

Timothy felt light and free, his heart no longer held down by the pain of the past. The truth had been difficult to hear, yes, but at least he was free of it all.

"Goodness," Lady Newfield murmured as they

walked out of the front door and stopped next to the carriage. "I certainly did not expect..."

"Nor did I," Timothy replied as Miss Mullins smiled a little wryly. "But at least we know the truth of the matter."

Miss Mullins touched his hand. "What do you think will happen now?" she asked, looking a little troubled. "Lady Parrington will surely not be allowed to continue?" She bit her lip. "What I mean to say is, do you think Lord Chesterton will continue to do as his sister demands, out of fear that she will reveal the truth of his misdemeanors?"

Considering for a moment, Timothy shook his head. "No, I think the strength of her hold over her brother and her husband has come to an end," he told her, seeing how the worry fled from her gaze. "There is nothing we need fear, Miss Mullins. And," he added, as an afterthought, "even if I am never entirely freed of this stain, I shall not care a whit. Because now, Miss Mullins, I have everything I need in you."

She blushed furiously but held onto his hand with both of her own, looking up at him with such love in her eyes that he wanted to pull her to him and kiss her with all the passion that was burning furiously within him.

"I think," Lady Newfield said, interrupting them, "that I shall walk for a short time." Smiling knowingly, she lifted a brow. "You will not mind taking your betrothed back to her uncle's townhouse, Lord Coventry?"

"Not in the least," he breathed as Miss Mullins giggled and embraced her godmother. "Miss Mullins, shall we?" He offered her his hand and she took it at once, climbing into the carriage and sitting down. When he climbed in after her, he did not sit opposite her but rather next to her, immediately wrapping one arm about her waist.

"Delilah," he breathed as she looked up into his face. "I am free at last."

Her eyes were fastened to his, searching his face. "And do you truly feel at ease?"

"More than I can say," he promised, his free hand finding hers. "Indeed, there is even a little sympathy in my heart for Lord Chesterton, even though I do not think that he chose the right path."

Miss Mullins shook her head. "Then I think all the more highly of you, Coventry," she told him, her fingers pressing his own. "For not every gentleman would feel such a thing."

Letting go of her hand, he touched her cheek. "I meant what I said in Miss Jamieson's dining room, Delilah. The affection I had—that I thought I had—for Lady Parrington is nothing compared to what I now have in my heart. I truly hope you know that."

"I believe it," she told him, her eyes glowing as she held his sincere gaze. "I see the truth of it in everything you do and say, in how you hold me and speak to me. Your affection is more and more apparent each day."

"It is more than a mere affection, Delilah," he said, feeling such a joy in his heart that he was finally able to speak to her so. "It is a love that has filled my heart so completely that it has shocked me thoroughly. I find myself aching for your company, desperate to be beside you again." Seeing how her smile softened, he pressed her hand again. "I love you desperately, Delilah. I never once expected this, never dreamt that I could feel such a thing, but now that it is here, I am grateful beyond explanation."

For a long moment, she said nothing. And then, her eyes sparkling like emeralds, she lifted her face to his and kissed him lightly on the lips. It was a mere brush, a gentle whisper, but it overpowered him completely.

A torrent of emotion crashed over Timothy, and, despite the awkwardness of the carriage, he found himself holding her tightly against him, kissing her lips again and again and feeling his heart burst with love.

"My heart is filled with none but you...Timothy," she whispered against his mouth. "You are the most honorable gentleman I have ever had the chance to meet, and no matter what lies before us, I shall never once step away from your side."

Cradling her face in his hands, Timothy closed his eyes and rested his forehead lightly against hers. "I love you, Delilah."

"As I love you."

I HOPE you enjoyed Delilah and Timothy's story! Don't miss the first book in the Convenient Arrangement series, A Broken Betrothal...Lady Augusta and Lord Leicestershire's arranged marriage becomes more than just business! Check out a preview just two pages ahead!

MY DEAR READER

Thank you for reading and supporting my books! I hope this story brought you some escape from the real world into the always captivating Regency world. A good story, especially one with a happy ending, just brightens your day and makes you feel good! If you enjoyed the book, would you leave a review on Amazon? Reviews are always appreciated.

Below is a complete list of all my books! Why not click and see if one of them can keep you entertained for a few hours?

The Duke's Daughters Series
The Duke's Daughters: A Sweet Regency Romance
Boxset
A Rogue for a Lady
My Restless Earl
Rescued by an Earl
In the Arms of an Earl
The Reluctant Marquess (Prequel)

A Smithfield Market Regency Romance
The Smithfield Market Romances: A Sweet Regency
Romance Boxset
The Rogue's Flower
Saved by the Scoundrel
Mending the Duke
The Baron's Malady

The Returned Lords of Grosvenor Square
The Returned Lords of Grosvenor Square: A Regency
Romance Boxset
The Waiting Bride
The Long Return
The Duke's Saving Grace
A New Home for the Duke

The Spinsters Guild
A New Beginning
The Disgraced Bride
A Gentleman's Revenge
A Foolish Wager
A Lord Undone

Convenient Arrangements
A Broken Betrothal
In Search of Love
Wed in Disgrace

Christmas Stories
Love and Christmas Wishes: Three Regency Romance
Novellas

A Family for Christmas
Mistletoe Magic: A Regency Romance
Home for Christmas Series Page

Happy Reading!

All my love,

Rose

A SNEAK PEAK OF A BROKEN
BETROTHAL

Lady Augusta looked at her reflection in the mirror and sighed inwardly. She had tried on almost every gown in her wardrobe and still was not at all decided on which one she ought to wear tonight. She had to make the right decision, given that this evening was to be her first outing into society since she had returned to London.

"Augusta, what in heaven's name...?" The sound of her mother's voice fading away as she looked all about the room and saw various gowns strewn everywhere, the maids quickening to stand straight, their heads bowed as the countess came into the room. Along with her came a friend of Lady Elmsworth, whom Augusta knew very well indeed, although it was rather embarrassing to have her step into the bedchamber when it was in such a disarray!

"Good afternoon, Mama," Augusta said, dropping into a quick curtsy. "And good afternoon, Lady Newfield." She took in Lady Newfield's face, seeing the twinkle in the lady's blue eyes and the way her lips twitched, which was in direct contrast to her mother, who was standing with her hands on her hips, clearly upset.

"Would you like to explain, my dear girl, what it is that you are doing here?" The countess looked into Augusta's face, her familiar dark eyes sharpening. Augusta tried to smile but her mother only narrowed her eyes and planted her hands on her hips, making it quite plain that she was greatly displeased with what Augusta was doing.

"Mama," Augusta wheedled, gesturing to her gowns. "You know that I must look my very best for this evening's ball. "Therefore, I must be certain that I—"

"We had already selected a gown, Augusta," Lady Elmsworth interrupted, quieting Augusta's excuses immediately. "You and I went to the dressmaker's only last week and purchased a few gowns that would be worn for this little Season. The first gown you were to wear was, if I recall, that primrose yellow." She indicated a gown that was draped over Augusta's bed, and Augusta felt heat rise into her face as the maids scurried to pick it up.

"I do not think it suits my coloring, Mama," she said, a little half-heartedly. "You are correct to state that we chose it together, but I have since reconsidered."

Lady Newfield cleared her throat, with Lady Elmsworth darting a quick look towards her.

"I would be inclined to agree, Lady Elmsworth," she said, only for Lady Elmsworth to throw up one hand, bringing her friend's words to a swift end. Augusta's hopes died away as her mother's thin brows began knitting together with displeasure. "That is enough, Augusta," she said firmly, ignoring Lady Newfield entirely. "That gown will do you very well, just as we discussed." She looked at the maids. "Tidy the rest of these up at once and ensure that the primrose yellow is left for this evening."

The maids curtsied and immediately set to their task, leaving Augusta to merely sit and watch as the maids obeyed the mistress of the house rather than doing what she wanted. In truth, the gown that had been chosen for her had been mostly her mother's choice, whilst she had attempted to make gentle protests that had mostly been ignored. With her dark brown hair and green eyes, Augusta was sure that the gown did, in fact, suit her coloring very well, but she did not want to be clad in yellow, not when so many other debutantes would be wearing the same. No, Augusta wanted to stand out, to be set apart, to be noticed! She had come to London only a few months ago for the Season and had been delighted when her father had encouraged them to return for the little Season. Thus, she had every expectation of finding a suitable husband and making a good match. However, given how particular her mother was being over her gown, Augusta began to worry that her mother would soon begin to choose Augusta's dance partners and the like so that she would have no independence whatsoever!

"I think I shall return to our tea," Lady Newfield said gently as Lady Elmsworth gave her friend a jerky nod. "I apologize for the intrusion, Lady Augusta."

"There was no intrusion," Augusta said quickly, seeing the small smile that ran around Lady Newfield's mouth and wishing that her mother had been a little more willing to listen to her friend's comments. For whatever reason, she felt as though Lady Newfield understood her reasoning more than her mother did.

"Now, Augusta," Lady Elmsworth said firmly, settling herself in a chair near to the hearth where a fire burned brightly, chasing away the chill of a damp winter afternoon. "This evening, you are to be introduced to one gentleman in particular. I want you to ensure that you behave impeccably. Greet him warmly and correctly, but thereafter, do not say a good deal."

Augusta frowned, her eyes searching her mother's face for answers that Lady Elmsworth was clearly unwilling to give. "Might I ask why I am to do such a thing, Mama?"

Lady Elmsworth held Augusta's gaze for a moment, and then let out a small sigh. "You will be displeased, of course, for you are always an ungrateful sort but nonetheless, you ought to find some contentment in this." She waited a moment as though waiting to see if Augusta had some retort prepared already, only to shrug and then continue. "Your father has found you a suitable match, Augusta. You are to meet him this evening."

The world seemed to stop completely as Augusta stared at her mother in horror. The footsteps of the maids came to silence; the quiet crackling of the fire turned to naught. Her chest heaved with great breaths as Augusta tried to accept what she had just been told, closing her eyes to shut out the view of her mother's slightly bored expression. This was not what she had expected. Coming back to London had been a matter of great excitement for her, having been told that *this* year would be the year for her to make a suitable match. She had never once thought that such a thing would be pulled from her, removed from her grasp entirely. Her father had never once mentioned that he would be doing such a thing but now, it seemed, he had chosen to do so without saying a word to her about his intentions.

"Do try to form some response, Augusta," Lady Elmsworth said tiredly. "I am aware this is something of a surprise, but it is for your own good. The gentleman in question has an excellent title and is quite wealthy." She waved a hand in front of her face as though such things were the only things in the world that mattered. "It is not as though you could have found someone on your own, Augusta."

"I should have liked the opportunity to try," Augusta whispered, hardly able to form the words she wanted so desperately to say.

"You had the summer Season," Lady Elmsworth retorted with a shrug. "Do you not recall?"

Augusta closed her eyes. The summer Season had been her first outing into society, and she had enjoyed every moment of it. Her father and mother had made it quite plain that this was not to be the year where she found a husband but rather a time for her to enjoy society, to become used to what it meant to live as a member of the *ton*. The little Season and the summer Season thereafter, she had been told, would be the ones for her to seek out a husband.

And now, that had been pulled away from her before she had even had the opportunity to be amongst the gentlemen of the *beau monde*.

"As I have said," Lady Elmsworth continued, briskly, ignoring Augusta's complaint and the clear expression of shock on her face, "there is no need for you to do anything other than dress in the gown we chose together and then to ensure that you greet Lord Pendleton with all refinement and propriety."

Augusta closed her eyes. "Lord Pendleton?" she repeated, tremulously, already afraid that this gentleman was some older, wealthy gentleman who, for whatever reason, had not been able to find a wife and thus had been more than eager to accept her father's offer.

"Did I not say?" Lady Elmsworth replied, sounding somewhat distracted. She rose quickly, her skirts swishing noisily as she walked towards the door. "He is brother to the Marquess of Leicestershire. A fine gentleman, by all accounts." She shrugged. "He is quiet and perhaps a little dull, but he will do very well for you." One of the maids held the door open, and before Augusta could say more, her mother swept out of the room and the door was closed tightly behind her.

Augusta waited for tears to come but they did not even begin to make their way towards her eyes. She was numb all over, cold and afraid of what was to come. This was not something she had even considered a possibility when it came to her own considerations for what the little Season would hold. There had always been the belief that she would be able to dance, converse, and laugh with as many gentlemen as thought to seek her out. In time, there would be courtships and one gentleman in particular might bring themselves to her notice. There would be excitement and anticipation, nights spent reading and re-reading notes and letters from the gentleman in question, her heart quickening at the thought of marrying him.

But now, such thoughts were gone from her. There was to be none of what she had expected, what she had hoped for. Instead, there was to be a meeting and an arrangement, with no passion or excitement.

Augusta closed her eyes and finally felt a sting of tears. Dropping her head into her hands, she let her emotions roar to life, sending waves of feeling crashing through her until, finally, Augusta wept.

CHAPTER ONE

Q uite why he had arranged to be present this evening, Stephen did not know. He ought to have stated that he would meet Lady Augusta in a quieter setting than a ball so that he might have talked with her at length rather than forcing a quick meeting upon them both in a room where it was difficult to hear one's own voice such was the hubbub of the crowd.

He sighed and looked all about him again, finding no delight in being in the midst of society once more. He was a somewhat retiring gentleman, finding no pleasure in the gossip and rumors that flung themselves all around London during the little Season, although it was always much worse during the summer Season. Nor did he appreciate the falseness of those who came to speak and converse with him, knowing full well that the only reason they did so was to enquire after his brother, the Marquess of Leicestershire.

His brother was quite the opposite in both looks and

character, for where Stephen had light brown hair with blue eyes, his brother had almost black hair with dark brown eyes that seemed to pierce into the very soul of whomever he was speaking with. The ladies of the *ton* wanted nothing more than to be in the presence of Lord Leicestershire and, given he was absent from society, they therefore came towards Stephen in order to find out what they could about his brother.

It was all quite wearisome, and Stephen did not enjoy even a moment of it. He was not as important as his brother, he knew, given he did not hold the high title nor have the same amount of wealth as Lord Leicestershire, but surely his own self, his conversation and the like, was of *some* interest? He grinned wryly to himself as he picked up a glass from the tray held by a footman, wondering silently to himself that, if he began to behave as his brother had done on so many occasions, whether or not that would garner him a little more interest from rest of the *ton*.

"You look much too contented," said a familiar voice, and Stephen looked to his left to see his acquaintance, Lord Dryden, approach him. Lord Dryden, a viscount, had an estate near the border to Scotland and, whilst lower in title than Stephen, had become something of a close acquaintance these last two years.

"Lord Dryden," Stephen grinned, slapping the gentleman on the back. "How very good to see you again."

Lord Dryden chuckled. "And you," he said with an honest look in his eyes. "Now, tell me why you are standing here smiling to yourself when I know very well that a ball is not the sort of event you wish to attend?"

Stephen's grin remained on his lips, his eyes alighting on various young ladies that swirled around him. "I was merely considering what my life might be like if I chose to live as my brother does," he answered, with a shrug. "I should have all of society chasing after me, I suppose, although a good many would turn their heads away from me with the shame of being in my company."

"That is quite true," Lord Dryden agreed, no smile on his face but rather a look of concern. "You do not wish to behave so, I hope?"

"No, indeed, I do not," Stephen answered firmly, his smile fading away. "I confess that I am growing weary of so many in the *ton* coming to seek me out simply because they wish to know more about my brother."

"He is not present this evening?"

Stephen snorted. "He is not present for the little Season," he replied with a shrug of his shoulders. "Do not ask me what he has been doing, or why he has such a notable absence, for I fear I cannot tell you." Setting his shoulders, he let out a long breath. "No, I must look to my future."

"Indeed," Lord Dryden responded, an interested look on his face as he eyed Stephen speculatively. "And what is it about your future that you now consider?"

Stephen cleared his throat, wondering whether he ought to tell his friend even though such an arrangement had not yet been completely finalized. "I am to consider myself betrothed very soon," he said before he lost his nerve and kept such news to himself. "I am to meet the lady here this evening. Her father has already signed the papers and they await me in my study." He shrugged one shoulder. "I am sure that, provided she has not lost all of her teeth and that her voice is pleasant enough, the betrothal will go ahead as intended."

Lord Dryden stared at Stephen for a few moments, visible shock rippling over his features. His eyes were wide and his jaw slack, without even a single flicker of mirth in his gaze as he looked back at him. Stephen felt his stomach drop, now worried that Lord Dryden would make some remark that would then force Stephen to reconsider all that he had decided thus far, fearful now that he had made some foolish mistake.

"Good gracious!" Lord Dryden began to laugh, his hand grasping Stephen's shoulder tightly. "You are betrothed?" Shaking his head, he let out another wheezing laugh before straightening and looking Stephen directly in the eye. "I should have expected such a thing from you, I suppose, given you are always entirely practical and very well-considered, but I had not expected it so soon!"

"So soon?" Stephen retorted with a chuckle. "I have been in London for the last three Seasons and have found not even a single young lady to be interested in even conversing with me without needing to talk solely about my brother." His lip curled, a heaviness sitting back on his shoulders as he let out a long sigh. "Therefore, this seemed to be the wisest and the most practical of agreements."

Lord Dryden chuckled again, his eyes still filled with good humor. "I am glad to hear it," he said warmly. "I do

congratulate you, of course! Pray, forgive me for my
humor. It is only that it has come as something of a
surprise to hear such a thing from you yet, now that I
consider it, it makes a good deal of sense!" He chuckled
again and the sound began to grate on Stephen, making
him frown as he returned his friend's sharp look.

Lord Dryden did not appear to care, even if he did
notice Stephen's ire. Instead, he leaned a little closer, his
eyes bright with curiosity. "Pray, tell me," he began as
Stephen nodded, resigning himself to a good many questions. "Who is this lady? Is she of good quality?"

"Very good, yes," Stephen replied, aware, while he
did not know the lady's features or character, that she
came from a good family line and that breeding would
not be a cause for concern. "She is Lady Augusta,
daughter to the Earl of Elmsworth."

Lord Dryden's eyes widened, and his smile faded for
a moment. "Goodness," he said quietly, looking at
Stephen as though he feared his friend had made some
sort of dreadful mistake. "And you have met the lady in
question?"

"I am to meet her this evening," Stephen answered
quickly, wondering why Lord Dryden now appeared so
surprised. "I have not heard anything disreputable about
her, however." He narrowed his gaze and looked at his
friend sharply. "Why? Have you heard some rumor I
have not?"

Lord Dryden held up both his hands in a gesture of
defense. "No, indeed not!" he exclaimed, sounding quite
horrified. "No, tis only that she is a lady who is very well
thought of in society. She is well known to everyone,

seeks to converse with them all, and has a good many admirers." One shoulder lifted in a half shrug. "To know that her father has sought out an arrangement for her surprises me a little, that is all."

"Because she could do very well without requiring an arrangement," Stephen said slowly understanding what Lord Dryden meant. "Her father appeared to be quite eager to arrange such a thing, however." He sighed and looked all about him, wondering when Lord Elmsworth and his daughter would appear. "He and I spoke at Whites when the matter of his daughter came up."

"And the arrangement came from there?" Lord Dryden asked as Stephen nodded. "I see." He lapsed into silence for a moment, then nodded as though satisfied that he had asked all the questions he wished. "Very good. Then may I be the first to congratulate you!" Lord Dryden's smile returned, and he held out a hand for Stephen to shake. Stephen did so after only a momentary hesitation, reminding himself that there was not, as yet, a complete agreement between himself and Lord Elmsworth.

"I still have to sign and return the papers," he reminded Lord Dryden, who made a noise in the back of his throat before shrugging. "You do not think there will be any difficulty there, I presume?"

"Of course there will not be any difficulty," Lord Dryden retorted with a roll of his eyes. "Lady Augusta is very pleasing, indeed. I am sure you will have no partic-ular difficulty with her."

Stephen opened his mouth to respond, only to see someone begin to approach him. His heart quickened in his chest as he looked at them a little more carefully, seeing Lord Elmsworth approaching and, with him, a young lady wearing a primrose yellow gown. She had an elegant and slender figure and was walking in a most demure fashion, with eyes that lingered somewhere near his knees rather than looking up into people's faces. Her dark brown hair was pulled away from her face, with one or two small ringlets tumbling down near her temples, so as to soften the severity of it. When she dared a glance at him, he was certain he caught a hint of emerald green in her eyes. Almost immediately, her gaze returned to the floor as she dropped into a curtsy, Lord Elmsworth only a step or two in front of her.

"Lord Pendleton!" Lord Elmsworth exclaimed, shaking Stephen's hand with great enthusiasm. "Might I present my daughter, Lady Augusta." He beamed at his daughter, who was only just rising from what had been a perfect curtsy.

"Good evening, Lady Augusta," Stephen said, bowing before her. "I presume your father has already made quite plain who I am?" He looked keenly into her face, and when she lifted her eyes to his, he felt something strike at his heart.

It was not warmth, however, nor a joy that she was quietly beautiful. It did not chime with happiness or contentment but rather with a warning. A warning that Lady Augusta was not as pleased with this arrangement as he. A warning that he might come to trouble if he continued as had been decided. She was looking at him with a hardness in her gaze that hit him hard. There was a coldness, a reserve in her expression, that he could not escape. Clearly, Lady Augusta was not at all contented with the arrangement her father had made for her, which, in turn, did not bode well for him.

"Yes," Lady Augusta said after a moment or two, her voice just as icy as her expression. "Yes, my father has informed of who you are, Lord Pendleton." She looked away, her chin lifted, clearly finding there to be no desire otherwise to say anything more.

Stephen cleared his throat, glancing towards Lord Dryden, who was, to his surprise, not watching Lady Augusta as he had expected, but rather had his attention focused solely on Lord Elmsworth. There was a dark frown on his face; his eyes narrowed just a little and a clear dislike began to ripple across his expression. What was it that Lord Dryden could see that Stephen himself could not?

"Might I introduce Viscount Dryden?" he said quickly, before he could fail in his duties. "Viscount Dryden, this is the Earl of Elmsworth and his daughter—"

"We are already acquainted," Lord Dryden interrupted, bowing low before lifting his head, looking nowhere but at Lady Augusta. "It is very pleasant to see you again, Lady Augusta. I hope you are enjoying the start of the little Season."

Something in her expression softened, and Stephen saw Lady Augusta's mouth curve into a gentle smile. She answered Lord Dryden politely and Stephen soon found himself growing a little embarrassed at the easy flow of conversation between his friend and his betrothed. There was not that ease of manner within himself, he realized, dropping his head just a little so as to regain his sense of composure.

"Perhaps I might excuse myself for a short time," Lord Elmsworth interrupted before Lord Dryden could ask Lady Augusta another question. "Lady Elmsworth is standing but a short distance away and will be watching my daughter closely."

Stephen glanced to his right and saw an older lady looking directly at him, her sense of haughtiness rushing towards him like a gust of wind. There was no content-ment in her eyes, but equally, there was no dislike either. Rather, there was the simple expectation that this was how things were to be done and that they ought to continue without delay.

"But of course, Lord Elmsworth," Stephen said quickly, bowing slightly. "I should like to sign your daughter's dance card, if I may?"

"I think," came Lady Augusta's voice, sharp and brittle, "then if that is the case, you ought to be asking the lady herself whether or not she has any space remaining on her card for you to do such a thing, Lord Pendleton."

There came an immediate flush of embarrassment onto Stephen's face, and he cleared his throat whilst Lord Elmsworth sent a hard glance towards his daughter, which she ignored completely. Only Lord Dryden chuck-led, the sound breaking the tension and shattering it into a thousand pieces as Stephen looked away.

"You are quite correct to state such a thing, Lady Augusta," Lord Dryden said, easily. "You must forgive my friend. I believe he was a little apprehensive about this meeting and perhaps has forgotten quite how things are done."

Stephen's smile was taut, but he forced it to his lips regardless. "But of course, Lady Augusta," he said tightly. "Might you inform me whether or not you have any spaces on your dance card that I might then be able to take from you?" He bowed his head and waited for her to respond, seeing Lord Elmsworth move away from them all without waiting to see what his daughter would say.

"I thank you for your kind consideration in requesting such a thing from me," Lady Augusta answered, a little too saucily for his liking. "Yes, I believe I do have a few spaces, Lord Pendleton. Please, choose whichever you like." She handed him her dance card and then pulled her hand back, the ribbon sliding from her wrist as he looked down at it. She turned her head away as if she did not want to see where he wrote his name, and this, in itself, sent a flurry of anger down Stephen's spine. What was wrong with this young lady? Was she not glad that she was now betrothed, that she would soon have a husband and become mistress of his estate?

For a moment, he wondered if he had made a mistake in agreeing to this betrothal, feeling a swell of relief in his chest that he had not yet signed the agreement, only for Lord Dryden to give him a tiny nudge, making him realize he had not yet written his name down on the dance card but was, in fact, simply staring at it as though it might provide him with all the answers he required.

"The country dance, mayhap," he said, a little more loudly than he had intended. "Would that satisfy you, Lady Augusta?"

She turned her head and gave him a cool look, no smile gracing her lips. "But of course," she said with more sweetness than he had expected. "I would be glad to dance with you, Lord Pendleton. The country dance sounds quite wonderful."

He frowned, holding her gaze for a moment longer before dropping his eyes back to her dance card again and writing his name there. Handing it back to her, he waited for her to smile, to acknowledge what he had given her, only for her to sniff, bob a curtsy and turn away. Stephen's jaw worked furiously, but he remained standing steadfastly watching after her, refusing to allow himself to chase after her and demand to know what she meant by such behavior. Instead, he kept his head lifted and his eyes fixed, thinking to himself that he had, most likely, made a mistake.

"I would ascertain from her behavior that this betrothal has come as something of a shock," Lord Dryden murmured, coming closer to Stephen and looking after Lady Augusta with interest. "She was less than pleased to be introduced to you, that is for certain!"

Stephen blew out his frustration in a long breath, turning his eyes away from Lady Augusta and looking at his friend. "I think I have made a mistake," he said gruffly. "That young lady will not do at all! She is—"

"She is overcome," Lord Dryden interrupted, holding up one hand to stem the protest from Stephen's lips. "As I have said, I think this has been something of a shock to her. You may recall that I said I am acquainted with Lady Augusta already and I know that how she presented herself this evening is not her usual character."

Stephen shook his head, his lips twisting as he considered what he was to do. "I am not certain that I have made the wisest decision," he said softly. "Obviously, I require a wife and that does mean that I shall have to select someone from amongst the *ton,* but—"

"Lady Augusta is quite suitable," Lord Dryden interrupted firmly. "And, if you were quite honest with yourself, Lord Pendleton, I think you would find that such an arrangement suits you very well. After all—" He gestured to the other guests around him. "You are not at all inclined to go out amongst the *ton* and find a lady of your choosing, are you?"

Stephen sighed heavily and shot Lord Dryden a wry look. "That is true enough, I suppose."

"Then trust me when I say that Lady Augusta is more than suitable for you," Lord Dryden said again, with such fervor that Stephen felt as though he had no other choice to believe him. "Sign the betrothal agreement and know that Lady Augusta will not be as cold towards you in your marriage as she has been this evening." He chuckled and slapped Stephen on the shoulder. "May I be the first to offer you my congratulations."

Smiling a little wryly, Stephen found himself nodding. "Very well," he told Lord Dryden. "I accept your congratulations with every intention of signing the betrothal agreement when I return home this evening."

"Capital!" Lord Dryden boomed, looking quite satisfied with himself. "Then I look forward to attending your wedding in the knowledge that it was I who brought it about." He chuckled and then, spotting a young lady coming towards him quickly excused himself. Stephen smiled as he saw Lord Dryden offer his arm to the young lady and then step out on to the floor. His friend was correct. Lady Augusta was, perhaps, a little overwhelmed with all that had occurred and simply was not yet open to the fact that she would soon be his wife. In time, she would come to be quite happy with him and their life together; he was sure of it. He had to thrust his worries aside and accept his decisions for what they were.

"I shall sign it the moment I return home," he said aloud to himself as though confirming this was precisely what he intended to do. With a small sigh of relief at his decision, he lifted his chin and set his shoulders. Within the week, everyone would know of his betrothal to Lady Augusta and that, he decided, brought him a good deal of satisfaction.

His QUILL HOVERED over the line for just a moment but, with a clenching of his jaw, Stephen signed his name on the agreement. His breath shot out of him with great fury, leaving him swallowing hard, realizing what he had done. It was now finalized. He would marry Lady Augusta, and the banns would have to be called very soon, given her father wanted her wed before the end of the little Season. Letting out his breath slowly, he rolled up the papers and began to prepare his seal, only for there to come a hurried knock at the door. He did not even manage to call out for his servant to enter, for the butler rushed in before he could open his mouth.

"Do forgive me, my lord," the butler exclaimed, breathing hard from his clear eagerness to reach Stephen in time. "This came from your brother's estate with a most urgent request that you read it at once."

Startled, his stomach twisting one way and then the other, Stephen took the note from the butler's hand and opened it, noting that there was no print on the seal. His heart began to pound as he read the news held within.

"My brother is dead," he whispered, one hand gripping onto the edge of his desk for support. "He...he was shot in a duel and died on the field." Closing his eyes, Stephen let the news wash over him, feeling all manner of strong emotions as he fought to understand what had occurred. His brother had passed away, then, lost to the grave, and out of nothing more than his foolishness. To have been fighting in a duel meant that Leicestershire had done something of the most grievous nature— whether it had been stealing another man's wife or taking affections from some unfortunate young lady without any intention of pursuing the matter further.

Running one hand over his face, Stephen felt the weight of his grief come to settle on his heart, his whole body seeming to ache with a pain he had only experienced once before when their dear father had passed away. His throat constricted as he thought of his mother. He would have to go to her at once, to comfort her in the midst of her sorrow. Yes, his brother had packed her off to the Dower House long before she was due to reside there, and yes, there had been some difficulties between them, but Stephen knew that she had loved her eldest son and would mourn the loss of him greatly.

A groan came from his lips as he lifted his head and tried to focus on his butler. His vision was blurry, his head feeling heavy and painful.

"Ready my carriage at once," he rasped, "and have my things sent after me. I must return to my brother's estate."

The butler bowed. "At once," he said, his concern clear in his wide-eyed expression. "I beg your pardon for my intrusion, my lord, but is Lord Leicestershire quite well?"

Stephen looked at his faithful butler, knowing that the man had worked for the family for many years in keeping the townhouse in London readied for them and understood that his concern was genuine. "My brother is dead," he said hoarsely as the butler gasped in horror. "I have lost him. He is gone, and I shall never see him again."

CHAPTER TWO

S*ix months later*

AUGUSTA ROLLED her eyes as her mother brought out the primrose yellow dress that she had worn at the start of the little Season some six months ago. She sighed as her mother spread it out with one hand, a look in her eye that told Augusta she was not about to escape this easily.

"That gown was for the winter, Mama," she said, calmly. "I cannot wear it again now that the sun is shining and the air is so very warm." She gestured to it with a look of what she hoped was sadness on her face. "Besides, it is not quite up to the fashion for this current Season."

Her mother tutted. "Nonsense, Augusta," she said briskly. "There is very little need for you to purchase new gowns when you are to have a trousseau. Your betrothed has, as you know, recently lost his brother and as such, will need to find some happiness in all that he does. I must hope that your presence will bring him a little joy in his sorrow and, in wearing the very same gown as you were first introduced to him in, I am certain that Lord Pendleton—I mean, Lord Leicestershire—will be very happy to see you again."

Augusta said nothing, silently disagreeing with her mother and having no desire whatsoever to greet her betrothed again, whether in her primrose yellow gown or another gown entirely. She had felt compassion and sympathy for his loss, yes, but she had silently reveled in her newfound freedom. Indeed, given their betrothal had not yet been confirmed and given the *ton* knew nothing of it, Augusta had spent the rest of the little Season enjoying herself, silently ignoring the knowledge that within the next few months, she would have to let everyone in the *ton* know of her engagement.

But not yet, it seemed. She had spoken to her father, and he had confirmed that the papers had not been returned by Lord Leicestershire but had urged her not to lose hope, stating that he had every reason to expect the gentleman to do just as he had promised but that he was permitting him to have some time to work through his grief before pressing him about the arrangement.

And when news had been brought that the new Marquess of Leicestershire had come to London for the Season, her father had taken it as confirmation that all was just as it ought to be. He was quite contented with the situation as things stood, silently certain that when Lord Leicestershire was ready, he would approach the Earl himself or speak directly to Augusta.

"I will not wear that gown, Mama," Augusta said frostily. "I am well aware of what you hope for but I cannot agree. That gown is not at all suitable for Lord Stonington's ball! I must find something that is quite beautiful, Mama." She saw her mother frown and tried quickly to come up with some reason for her to agree to such a change. "I know your intentions are good," she continued, swiftly, "but Lord Leicestershire will be glad to see me again no matter what I am wearing; I am sure of it. And, Mama, if I wear the primrose yellow gown, might it not remind him of the night that he was told of his brother's death?" She let her voice drop low, her eyes lowering dramatically. "The night when he had no other choice but to run from London so that he might comfort his mother and tidy up the ruin his brother left behind."

"Augusta!" Lady Elmsworth's voice was sharp. "Do not speak in such a callous manner!"

Augusta, who was nothing if not practical, looked at her mother askance. "I do not consider speaking the truth plainly to be callous, Mama," she said quite calmly. "After all, it is not as though Lord Leicestershire's brother was anything other than a scoundrel." She shrugged, turning away from her mother and ignoring the horrified look on her face. "Everyone in London is well aware what occurred."

She herself had been unable to escape the gossip and, to her shame, had listened to it eagerly at times. The late Lord Leicestershire had lost his life in a duel that had not gone well for him. He had taken a young lady of quality and attempted to steal kisses—and perhaps more—from her, only to be discovered by the young lady's brother, who was a viscount of some description. Despite the fact that such duels were frowned upon, one had taken place and the gentleman who had done such a dreadful thing to a young lady of society had paid the ultimate price for his actions. A part of her did feel very sorry indeed for the newly titled Lord Leicestershire, knowing that he must have had to endure a good deal of struggle, difficulty and pain in realizing not only what his brother had done but in taking on all the responsibilities that now came with his new title.

"I should think you better than to listen to gossip," Lady Elmsworth said, primly. "Now, Augusta, do stop being difficult and wear what I ask of you."

"No," Augusta replied quite firmly, surprising both herself and her mother with her vehemence. "No, I shall not." Taking in the look of astonishment on her mother's face, Augusta felt her spirits lift very high indeed as she realized that, if she spoke with determination, her mother might, in fact, allow her to do as she wished. She had, thus far, always bowed to her mother's authority, but ever since she had discovered that her marriage was already planned for her and that she was to have no independence whatsoever, she had found a small spark growing steadily within her. A spark that determined that she find some way to have a little autonomy, even if it would only be for a short time.

"I will wear the light green silk," she said decisively, walking to her wardrobe and indicating which one she meant. "It brings out my complexion a little more, I think." She smiled to herself and touched the fabric gently. "And I believe it brings a little more attention to my eyes."

Lady Elmsworth sighed heavily but, thankfully, she set down the primrose yellow and then proceeded to seat herself in a chair by the fire, which was not lit today given the warmth of the afternoon. "You think this is the most suitable choice, then?"

"I do," Augusta said firmly. "I shall wear this and have a few pearls and perhaps a ribbon set into my hair." Again, she smiled but did not see her mother's dark frown. "And perhaps that beautiful diamond pendant around my neck."

Lady Elmsworth's frown deepened. "You need not try to draw attention to yourself, Augusta," she reminded her sternly. "You are betrothed. You will be wed to Lord Leicestershire and he is the only one you need attempt to impress."

Augusta hid the sigh from her mother as she turned back to her wardrobe, closing the door carefully so as not to crush any of her gowns. A part of her hoped that she would not have to marry Lord Leicestershire, for given he had not yet returned the betrothal agreement to her father, there seemed to be no eagerness on his part to do so or to proceed with their engagement. Mayhap, now that he was of a great and high title, he might find himself a little more interested in the young ladies of the *ton* and would not feel the need to sign the betrothal agreement at all. It might all come to a very satisfactory close, and she could have the freedom she had always expected.

"Augusta!" Lady Elmsworth's voice was sharp, as though she knew precisely what it was Augusta was thinking. "You will make sure that all of your attention is on your betrothed this evening. Do you understand me?"

"We are not betrothed yet, Mama," Augusta replied a little tartly. "Therefore, I cannot show him any specific attention for fear of what others might say." She arched one eyebrow and looked at her mother as she turned around, aware she was irritating her parent but finding a dull sense of satisfaction in her chest. "Once the agreement has been sent to Papa, then, of course, I shall do my duty." She dropped into a quick curtsy, her eyes low and her expression demure, but it did not fool Lady Elmsworth.

"You had best be very careful with your behavior this evening, Augusta," she exclaimed, practically throwing herself from her chair as she rose to her feet, her cheeks a little pink and her eyes blazing with an unexpressed frustration. "I shall be watching you most carefully."

"Of course, Mama," Augusta replied quietly, permitting herself a small smile as her mother left the room, clearly more than a little irritated with all that Augusta had said. Augusta let a long breath escape her, feeling a sense of anticipation and anxiety swirl all about within her as she considered what was to come this evening. Lord Leicestershire would be present, she knew, for whilst he had not written to her directly to say such a thing, all of London was abuzz with the news that the new Marquess had sent his acceptance to Lord Stonington's ball. Everyone would want to look at him, to see his face and to wonder just how like his brother he might prove to be. Everyone, of course, except for Augusta. She would greet him politely, of course, but had no intention of showing any interest in him whatsoever. Perhaps that, combined with his new title and his new appreciation from the *ton,* might decide that she was no longer a suitable choice for a wife.

Augusta could only hope.

～

"Good evening, Lady Augusta."

Augusta gasped in surprise as she turned to see who had spoken her name, before throwing herself into the arms of a lovely lady. "Lady Mary!" she cried, delighted to see her dear friend again. They had shared one Season already as debutantes and had become very dear friends indeed, and Augusta had missed her at the little Season. "How very glad I am to see you again. I am in desperate need of company and you have presented yourself to me at the very moment that I need you!"

Lady Mary laughed and squeezed Augusta's hand. "But of course," she said, a twinkle in her eye. "I knew very well that you would need a dear friend to walk through this Season with you—just as I need one also!" She turned and looked at the room, the swirling colors of the gowns moving all around them, and let out a contented sigh. "I am quite certain that this Season, we shall both find a suitable match, and I, for one, am eagerly looking forward to the courtship, the excitement and the wonderfulness that is sure to follow!"

Augusta could not join in with the delight that Lady Mary expressed, her heart suddenly heavy and weighted as it dropped in her chest. Lady Mary noticed at once, her joyous smile fading as she looked into Augusta's face.

"My dear friend, whatever is the matter?"

Augusta opened her mouth to answer, only for her gaze to snag on something. Or, rather, a familiar face that seemed to loom out of the crowd towards her, her heart slamming hard as she realized who it was.

"Lady Augusta?"

Lady Mary's voice seemed to be coming from very far away as Augusta's eyes fixed upon Lord Leicestershire, her throat constricting and a sudden pain stabbing into her chest. He was standing a short distance away, and even though there were other guests coming in and out of her vision, blocking her view of him entirely upon occasion, she seemed to be able to see him quite clearly. His eyes were fixed to hers, appearing narrowed and dark and filled with nothing akin to either gladness or relief upon seeing her. Her stomach dropped to the floor for an inexplicable reason, making her wonder if he felt the same about her as she did about him. Why did that trouble her, she wondered, unable to tug her gaze from his. She should be able to turn her head away from him at once, should be able to show the same disregard as she had done at their first meeting, should be able to express her same dislike for their arrangement as she had done at the first—but for whatever reason, she was not able to do it.

"Lady Augusta, you are troubling me now!"

Lady Mary's voice slowly came back to her ears, growing steadily louder until the hubbub of the room appeared to be much louder than before. She closed her eyes tightly, finally freed from Lord Leicestershire's gaze, and felt her whole body tremble with a strange shudder.

"Lady Mary," she breathed, her hand touching her friend's arm. "I—I apologize. It is only that I have seen my betrothed and I—"

"Your betrothed?"

Lady Mary's eyes widened, her cheeks rapidly losing their color as she stared at Augusta with evident concern.

"You are engaged?" Lady Mary whispered as Augusta's throat tightened all the more. "When did such a thing occur?"

Augusta shook her head minutely. "It was not something of my choosing," she answered hoarsely. "My father arranged it on my behalf, without my knowledge of it. When I was present in the little Season, I was introduced to Lord Pendleton."

"Lord Pendleton?" Lady Mary exclaimed, only to close her eyes in embarrassment and drop her head.

Augusta smiled tightly. "Indeed," she said, seeing her friend's reaction and fully expecting her to be aware of the situation regarding Lord Pendleton. "He has not signed the betrothal agreement as far as I am aware, for it has not yet been returned to my father. However, given he has been in mourning for his brother, my father has not been overly eager in pursuing the matter, believing that Lord Leicestershire—as he is now—will return the papers when he is quite ready."

Lady Mary said nothing for some moments, considering all that had been said carefully and letting her eyes rove towards where Augusta had been looking towards only a few moments before.

"That is most extraordinary," she said, one hand now pressed against her heart. "And might I inquire as to whether or not you are pleased with this arrangement?"

With a wry smile, Augusta said nothing but looked at her friend with a slight lift of her eyebrow, making Lady Mary more than aware of precisely how she felt.

"I see," Lady Mary replied, her eyes still wide but seeming to fill with sympathy as she squeezed Augusta's hand, her lips thin. "I am sorry that you have had to endure such difficulties. I cannot imagine what you must have felt to be told that your marriage was all arranged without you having any awareness of such a thing beforehand!"

"It has been rather trying," Augusta admitted softly. "I have a slight hope through it all, however."

"Oh?"

Allowing herself another smile, Augusta dared a glance back towards Lord Leicestershire, only to see him still watching her. Embarrassed, she pulled her eyes away quickly, looking back to her friend. "I have a slight hope that he might decide *not* to sign the papers," she said as Lady Mary sucked in a breath. "As he is now a marquess and an heir, what if he decides that he must now choose his bride with a good deal more consideration?" Feeling a little more relaxed, no longer as anxious and as confused as she had been only a few moments before, she allowed herself a small smile. "I might be able to discover my freedom once more."

Lady Mary did not smile. Rather, her lips twisted to one side, and her brows lowered. "But would that not then mean that your father might, once again, find you another match of his choosing?" she said quietly, as though she were afraid to upset Augusta any further. "Lord Leicestershire is certainly an excellent match, Lady Augusta. He is a marquess and will have an excellent fortune. Surely he is not to be dismissed with such ease!"

Augusta allowed herself to frown, having not considered such a thing before. She did not want to be saddled with anyone of her father's choosing, instead wanting to discover a husband of her own choice. There was that choice there that, up until the previous little Season, she had always expected to have.

"I will simply speak to my father," she said airily, trying to express some sort of expectation that her father would do precisely what she asked. "He will be willing to listen to me, I am sure."

Lady Mary's expression cleared. "Well, if that is true, then I must hope that you can extricate yourself from this...if you so wish." That flickering frown remained, reminding Augusta that she was now betrothed to a marquess. A Marquess who had influence, wealth, and a high title. Was she being foolish hoping that the betrothal would come to an end? Did she truly value her own choice so much that she would throw aside something that so many others in society would pursue with everything they had?

"I..." Augusta trailed off, looking into her friend's eyes and knowing that, with Lady Mary, she had to be honest.

"I shall consider what you have said," she agreed eventually as Lady Mary's frown finally lifted completely. "You are right to state that he *is*, in fact, a marquess, and mayhap he is not a match that I should be so eager to thrust aside."

"Might I inquire as to how often you have been in his company?" Lady Mary asked, turning to stand beside Augusta so that she might look out through the ballroom a little better. "Do you know him *very* well? Does he have a difficult personality that makes your eagerness to wed him so displeasing?"

Augusta winced as a knowing look came into Lady Mary's eyes. "I confess that I have not spent any time with him at all," she admitted, "save for our introduction and, thereafter, a country dance." She lifted one shoulder in a half shrug whilst avoiding Lady Mary's gaze. "Perhaps I have been a little hasty."

Lady Mary chuckled and nodded. "Mayhap," she agreed, with a smile that lit up her expression. "He may very well be a very fine gentleman indeed, Lady Augusta, and soon, you will be considered the most fortunate of all the young ladies present in London for the Season."

As much as Augusta did not want to accept this, as much as she wanted to remain determined to make her own choice, she had to admit that Lady Mary had made some valid considerations and she ought to take some time to think through all that had been said. It was not with trepidation but with a sense of curiosity deep within her that she walked through the ballroom with Lady Mary by her side, ready to greet Lord Leicestershire again. There was a little more interest in her heart and mind now, wondering what he would say and how he would appear when he greeted her. With a deep breath,

she smiled brightly as she drew near him, her heart quickening just a little as she curtsied.

"Lord Leicestershire," she said, lifting her eyes to his
and noting, with a touch of alarm, that there was not even
a flicker of a smile touching his lips. "Good evening. How
very good to see you again."

Lord Leicestershire frowned, his brow furrowed and
his eyes shadowed. "Pardon me, my lady," he said as the
other gentlemen he was talking to turned their attention
towards both her and Lady Mary. "But I do not recall
your name. In fact," he continued, spreading his hands, "I
do not think we have ever been acquainted!"

Augusta's mouth dropped open in astonishment, her
eyes flaring wide and her cheeks hot with embarrassment
as she saw each of the gentlemen looking at her and then
glancing at each other with amusement. Lady Mary
gaped at Lord Leicestershire, her hand now on Augusta's
elbow.

"If you will excuse me," Augusta croaked, trying to
speak with strength only for her to practically whisper. "I
must..."

"You are due to dance," Lady Mary interjected, help-
fully guiding Augusta away from Lord Leicestershire.
"Come, Lady Augusta."

Augusta let her friend lead her from the group,
feeling utter humiliation wash all over her. Keeping her
head low, she allowed Lady Mary to guide her to the
opposite side of the room, silently praying that no one
else was watching her. Glancing from one side to the
other, she heard the whispers and laughter coming from
either side of her and closed her eyes tightly, fearful that

the rumors and gossip were already starting. For what-ever reason, Lord Leicestershire had either chosen to pretend he did not know her or truly had forgotten her, and either way, Augusta was completely humiliated.

WHAT HAPPENS next with Lady August and Lord Leicestershire? Will they continue to fight or will they find a way to respect each other? Check out the rest of the story in the Kindle Store A Broken Betrothal

Made in the USA
Middletown, DE
15 March 2021